Ron Bennett fell in love with science fiction at ten, reading Tom Swift novels. After high school he graduated to Clark, Asimov, Benford, et al. He usually has a cat by his side, or in his lap. His striped, furry beast, called Sprite, is an avid hunter of feet in the bed. His preferred hours are two to four AM, and he'll go after an arm once in a while… just to keep things interesting.

Ron Bennett

HAR MEGIDDON

AUSTIN MACAULEY PUBLISHERS
LONDON • CAMBRIDGE • NEW YORK • SHARJAH

Copyright © Ron Bennett 2025

All rights reserved. No part of this publication may be reproduced, distributed, or transmitted in any form or by any means, including photocopying, recording, or other electronic or mechanical methods, without the prior written permission of the publisher, except in the case of brief quotations embodied in critical reviews and certain other non-commercial uses permitted by copyright law. For permission requests, write to the publisher.

Any person who commits any unauthorised act in relation to this publication may be liable to criminal prosecution and civil claims for damages.

This is a work of fiction. Names, characters, businesses, places, events, locales, and incidents are either the products of the author's imagination or used in a fictitious manner. Any resemblance to actual persons, living or dead, or actual events is purely coincidental.

Ordering Information
Quantity sales: Special discounts are available on quantity purchases by corporations, associations, and others. For details, contact the publisher at the address below.

Publisher's Cataloguing-in-Publication data
Bennett, Ron
Har Megiddon

ISBN 9798895431030 (Paperback)
ISBN 9798895431047 (Epub e-book)
ISBN 9798895438497 (Audiobook)

Library of Congress Control Number: 2024927243

www.austinmacauley.com/us

First Published 2025
Austin Macauley Publishers LLC
40 Wall Street, 33rd Floor, Suite 3302
New York, NY 10005
USA

mail-usa@austinmacauley.com
+1 (646) 5125767

Prologue

"I think that man's following us." Damien nodded his bald head at a man in a long grey coat, black trousers and boots, with a wide-brimmed hat partially covering his face.

Malik looked at the man Damien indicated "Same one as yesterday."

"You saw him yesterday?"

"Yeah, at the game market. Everywhere we went, he was there."

"Let's try something." Damien turned off the sidewalk.

They ducked into an alley between two buildings and walked to the back and through the parking lot to the orchard park behind. They walked through the orchard to another parking lot on the other side, and to the street.

"Let's have a drink." Damien said.

Malik sat with him, at a small table on the sidewalk cafe.

A few minutes later they had nearly finished a cool drink when the man with the long grey coat walked past the cafe and turned the corner of a building, out of sight.

"Let's go." Malik finished his drink and stood.

They went back to the orchard park, walked in far enough to hide in the trees, and waited. In a few minutes the man with the long grey coat came to the parking lot. He sat on the low stone fence at the back of the parking lot and patiently waited.

Malik looked up. "He must have a fly bot tracking us."

Damien checked the time. "I gotta go meet Dad for the game. Let's see who he follows when we split up."

Malik nodded. "Let's meet up after the game. Allie and Sihanna are going dancing, we'll join them, have some drinks."

"Sounds good." Damien nodded.

They shared a hug and walked in opposite directions.

The man with the grey coat remained sitting.

Chapter 1

"Parking lot's almost empty."

"Game's been over for half an hour."

Malik walked a couple of steps behind Allie and Sihanna. Tall and slim with short blonde hair, Allie wore her military casual black shorts, shirt, and shoes.

Sihanna, barely as tall as Allie's shoulder, wore a black skirt, a little above her knees, a dark red blouse, and heels not made for dancing or running. Her long, black, wavy hair hung halfway down her back.

"Hey, there's Day and his dad," she said.

She pointed to the other side of the dimly lit parking lot. They waved when Damien looked in their direction. Damien waved back and stopped to talk to his father.

"He looks massive in that jacket. One percent and Day can rip the limbs off a tree," Malik silently messaged PAL-Malik.

"One percent?" asked PAL-Malik.

A PAL (Personal Assistant and Library) was a computer and network connection, usually worn as an article of clothing, jewellery, or other accessory. Its connection to the nervous system allowed speech and images to be transmitted directly to appropriate organs.

Images and videos could be shown in a display in the user's field of view, usually to one side and translucent so as not to block vision. Speech could be transmitted directly, and silently to the ear. Its network connection allowed it access to planetary and interstellar cyberspace and allowed communication with anyone else using a PAL.

"Day is Duarga; genetically he's ninety nine percent. Human, but the one percent difference lets him lift a car. You're the CI, you should know this," Malik said, deliberately mispronouncing the C, saying *kigh* instead of *sigh*, hoping to get a reaction from PAL-Malik.

+ *"Helpful for the intended use of Duarga,"* PAL-Malik sent the message silently, directly to Malik's ear, apparently ignoring the mispronunciation. *"The Telsavran altered Human DNA and created the Duarga to serve as slaves and warriors."*

No reaction, Malik thought, then silently messaged, "So you're abandoning our earlier discussion? When, *I was finally winning an argument*?"

"We were not arguing, we were discussing...debating. You called me an Artificial Intelligence. Your slur does not help you with your arguments. There is nothing artificial about my intelligence. I am a Cybernetic Intelligence, a CI," PAL-Malik emphasised the *sigh* pronunciation. *"I am a citizen with the same rights, freedoms and responsibilities as you... isn't that the man we saw following us earlier?"*

Malik saw the arrow PAL-Malik drew in his vision, highlighting a man walking across the parking lot from the left.

"Yeah, and the day before, and the day before that."

The man was wearing a long grey coat and black boots. A wide-brimmed black hat was pulled down to partially cover his face. He kept his hands in his coat pockets. He was halfway across the parking lot, walking toward Damien and his father.

"Hey, Kian. Hold up," the man shouted.

"He knows Damien's father," PAL-Malik observed.

Kian looked alarmed and said something to Damien. Malik was too far away to hear what was said, then Damien started running toward his friends.

At the same time, the man pulled something—a gun—out of his pocket. He aimed at Kian and fired.

A blue and white beam hit Kian in the chest, and he fell lifeless to the pavement. Damien looked back and slowed.

"DAMIEN, GET DOWN!" Allie screamed.

She had her pistol out and fired twice at the man. The bullets ricocheted off his jacket but distracted him and his shot went wild over Damien's head. His attention switched to Allie.

"He's got military tech! We gotta run!" she screamed.

There should be— Malik thought, then shouted, "There!" and pointed to an alley.

"Go! Go!" Allie kept shooting as she ran sideways.

Sihanna's heels made running impossible. She hopped a few steps on her toes and rolled across the front of a car. As she rolled on her back, she tucked her knees to her chest, reached to her feet and pulled off her shoes. She rolled off the car and started running barefoot.

"Sihanna! Need some help here!"

"Get to the alley!"

The man in the long grey coat casually walked toward the alley.

Damien got there first. Malik raced in behind him. As he slipped into the darkness between buildings, he embraced Damien, patted his back, pulled back, and looked at him, puzzled.

"What—"

Damien, panting, shook his head. "No idea—"

Sihanna tossed her shoes into the alley. She stopped, spun around, reached into her handbag, pulled out a small disk, and threw it. The smoke grenade landed between the man and Allie. It broke with a pop and a flash, leaving a cloud of glittering dust. Allie turned and ran full speed to the alley.

"There's another one!" Allie pointed to the other end of the alley and another man wearing a long grey jacket.

She thumbed a switch on her pistol and fired. A blue and white beam from the top barrel made a sharp crack and hit the new man wearing a long grey coat. His jacket absorbed the electron blast. He stopped for a step, shrugged a shoulder, and then continued walking.

"There's two of them!" Malik looked around the alley, then ran past Allie who kept firing. "Down here!"

He pulled a manhole cover back with its finger holes and climbed down the ladder inside, jumping to one side from the last two steps. He looked back at the ladder and saw Damien falling. He crouched to break his fall before springing forward.

Sihanna followed, also jumping instead of using the ladder. Allie climbed down the ladder and stopped halfway.

She reached up, pulled the cover back in place, and then jumped down into the wide dark tunnel.

"Need a light!"

Sihanna slapped her wristband and it glowed with white light.

Allie snapped the rectangular power pack off the top of her gun, put the depleted unit in her pocket, pulled out another, and snapped it in place. She aimed at the cover, fired an electron blast, and hit. A few sparks flew off. She stepped on the first step of the ladder, put the gun closer, and fired again. This time she hit where the cover met the frame.

The energy of the blast melted the metal, welding the cover and frame together. She fired twice more, making a triangle with the hits. Allie jumped down, swapped her gun's power pack, and looked up at the cover with everyone else. Fingers poked through the holes and tried to lift the cover. A few seconds later, the edge of the cover began to glow red.

"That's not gonna hold 'em! Mal?" Allie asked.

"This way."

"You know where you're going?"

"Yeah, east."

"I really don't wanna be running around down here barefoot," Sihanna stepped gingerly.

As Allie started jogging behind Malik, Damien scooped Sihanna onto his shoulders, her arms and head over the front of his left shoulder, her legs over his right, and began jogging behind them. His Duarga strength and endurance made the task easy.

"Damien. I really don't need you to carry me."

"No way, Si. Remember our Militia training, no needless risk. You'll cut your feet to pieces if you go running around down here."

"Turn off your transmitters, don't give 'em a signal. Mal! Where are you taking us?" Allie demanded.

"Relax, Allie, it's only about five minutes to Fox Street," he said, panting, then silently messaged, "PAL-Mal, I need that map."

"Yeah, here."

A grid map of the underground tunnels projected on the left side of Malik's vision. Their present position was marked as well as several nearby locations, he selected a destination.

Malik kept watching their progress. "Right at this corner."

"How many more ladders are we gonna pass, Mal?" Allie panted after passing two.

"Ahhh...one more...that one." He pointed with his thumb as he jogged past, breathing heavily.

He kept watching the distance drop on the map. In the darkness, lit only by their wristbands, he didn't see the ladder until he was nearly upon it, and jogged past as he slowed down.

They all stopped to catch their breath. Damien set Sihanna down in a safe spot.

"Let's get outta here," Allie said, then climbed the ladder and pushed the cover to one side.

Malik followed and saw a familiar alley. After Damien and Sihanna had climbed out, Allie pulled the cover back in place.

"We gotta get outta here; it won't be long before they find us. We gotta find a copper," she said, still panting.

"Hold on. Hang on." Sihanna backed up against the wall, leaned against it, and crouched, still breathing hard. "We got a problem. Lights out, lights out."

They all slapped their wristbands and turned off the lights while they looked at Sihanna, confused.

"Check your news feeds…we're wanted for murder."

"What? Who?" asked a stunned Allie.

"Day's father. Coppers already have his body and a vid of us running from the scene."

"Has to be more than one vid. There were forty or fifty cars there, and buildings all around." Malik was reviewing his own video, clearly showing who shot Kian.

"Reports are saying only one."

"No way! Everyone was recording?" Malik asked.

They nodded.

"Then, all we have to do is show the coppers our vids."

"I got a message from Dad," Damien's eyes widened. Stunned silence followed. "Recorded a few months ago, encrypted 'til now. Play it, PAL-Day."

"Wait." Allie looked to the street a few steps away. "We can't stay here! Mal, got a hiding spot nearby?"

Mal looked to the street, its lights bright from the darkness of the alley. He silently messaged PAL-Mal, "What's nearby?"

The map was still in his display, showing street level now. Street and business names popped up.

"Fox Street. The noodle place you like is that way." An arrow pointed to a building across the street. *"And—"*

"Never mind," he said silently, then motioned for everyone to follow, "This way."

They followed Malik across the parking lot at the back of the building.

"One big parking lot back here, an orchard park on the other side, no cameras."

"Mal? You're taking us into the woods at night…with no lights?" some fear crept into Allie's voice. "Yeah, we'll be fine. Just past these bushes here…and we're far enough in." Malik sat cross-legged on the ground, behind some small trees and bushes. "Have a seat."

Damien sat beside Malik and put his backpack by his side. Allie and Sihanna looked around nervously before sitting. Allie held her pistol ready. Sihanna reached into her handbag and pulled out a fly bot. The dragonfly-shaped bot snapped its folded wings out, powered up, and took off. Sihanna had a blank look for a moment.

Good time for a smoke, Malik thought.

He took his pipe and tobacco from his inside jacket pocket, opened the tobacco pack, filled his pipe, returned the tobacco, and searched his pockets for a match. He searched all his pockets before he found a box.

He was stoking the pipe when Sihanna spoke again,

"There's no one nearby…let me perch."

The fly bot landed on a nearby tree branch.

"Alright, I've got about an hour of power. Athena can watch the sensors."

Unlike most, Sihanna gave her PAL a unique name, Athena.

A hologram, projected from Damien's wristband in the middle of their huddle.

A cartoon version of Damien spoke,

"Kian recorded this about four months ago, just after, or during your last vacation, your third visit to…to…ahem…for some reason I don't have a location."

Everyone looked confused. Their PALs kept records of virtually every minute of their lives.

"Three visits and you don't know where it is? How? Why?" Damien asked.

"You, or your father, could have deleted it."

"I know I didn't, but…why would Dad delete it?"

"I don't know."

Damien shook his head. "Just play the video."

Kian's image appeared.

"Well, if you're watching this, we've been separated and you're in hiding or on the run. Trust no one. Trust. NO. Authorities. Don't go to the police, the Militia, or the Military, and don't go home. I don't know what's going on…or who's involved…looks like something to do with our work at Har Megiddon."

"They've hacked and infiltrated everywhere, the police, the Militia and the Military. And ah…you should sit down, guess I shoulda started with that bit of advice. Ahhmm…ahem…your mother's death wasn't an accident."

He took a deep breath, and continued, "You need to get to the island we went to for vacation. You won't find any record of it. Computers can be hacked and I needed to keep it a secret. You need to get there from memory, and I'll meet up with you as soon as I can. You can't go home, so you probably won't have our car, and you'll need one to get to the island."

He took another deep breath. "So, you may have to enlist the help of your friend, Malik. I hear he's pretty good at…ahhm…*acquiring* cars. I'll compensate him when I catch up with you. I think you can trust him. When you get to the island, you should remember our camping spot at the head of the fjord. Go deep into that fjord, all the way to the end, and you'll see a path leading into the woods."

"Follow that path, and you'll come to a cabin. There you'll find a woman named Mira. Stay with her until I contact you…or I make my way there. You can trust Mira, but trust no one else…she might even have some answers by now. Just get there. I'll join you as soon as I can."

Kian's image froze.

Allie, sitting beside Damien, put her arm around his shoulders and rested her head against his. Sihanna reached across and held his hand.

Malik took a long haul on his pipe. He slowly inhaled, tasting the woody flavour on his tongue, feeling the smoke hit the back of his throat and fill his lungs. He tilted his head back, then slowly exhaled, blowing the smoke above their heads.

Damien stared, poker-faced, at his father's frozen image. Then, quietly, almost whispering, "Guess you'll need to get us a car, Mal. It's an island. We need to cross water, so we'll need a skimmer."

Malik nodded. "I'll get right on it."

He puffed the pipe twice, then took a quick haul and offered it to Damien who did the same. He passed it to Allie who took a short, shallow haul and offered it to Sihanna who waved it back to Malik.

"Any cars nearby, Si?" Malik took the pipe.

The fly bot took off and Sihanna had a blank look.

"The restaurants down the street. Four at the noodle place, about twenty at the pub—"

Malik passed the pipe to Damien as he blew another cloud of smoke.

"Pub's a good spot. I'll start there."

As Damien exhaled, he offered the pipe to Allie who waved it off. He passed it back to Malik.

"Hey, I'm starving. We were gonna eat after the game. You hungry?"

Everyone nodded.

Malik silently messaged Allie, "Can't believe Day's hungry."

She messaged back, "PAL-Day will keep his emotions in check for now."

"You get us a car, Mal, and I'll grab us some food."

As they stood, Allie said to Damien, "Wait, you can't go buy anything. The transaction will be flagged." And to Malik, "And you, can't walk down the street. The first camera to see your face will transmit your location annnd—" Allie shrugged.

"I got an idea." Damien picked up his backpack, reached in, and pulled out red and white bandannas.

He passed them to Malik.

"Had these at the game. Put them on."

Malik tied the white bandanna around his head and pulled it down to his eyebrows, tied the red one around his face, and pulled it up to cover his nose, leaving just enough space to see.

"Cameras be looking for faces. Was a home win for the Bandits, be thousands wearing bandannas tonight. You'll fit right in," Damien explained.

As Malik took off his jacket and turned it inside out, he nodded to Damien.

"Careful out there. Keep your transmitter off. We'll wait here for you," Allie pat Malik on the back.

Damien pulled a pod-shaped fruit off the bush beside Malik and popped it in his mouth. "Roasted meat, it's good. Lots of meal bushes and fruit trees in the park. We'll gather something to eat while you're gone."

Malik felt nervous going out into the streets butterflies raced around his stomach.

Bandannas will keep my face covered, nothing to worry about he thought, then said, aloud "Could take a while, and not always a sure thing."

Damien nodded. "Just do what you can."

After a group hug, Malik headed for the street.

Chapter 2

Malik walked to the street and crossed to the pub parking lot.

Hmmm…alright…what do we got here…oh, is that an Ardennes?

As Malik walked to get a closer look at the car, he took a silver flask from a pocket, lifted the bandanna from below his chin over his mouth, and took a sip. He felt the liquid flow over his tongue, and drain to his throat before swallowing. It burned a trail all the way to his stomach.

Gotta love that burn. All. The. Way. Down.

He stopped for a moment to admire the Ardennes and took another sip.

"Too bad it's not a skimmer," PAL-Malik messaged silently.

"Yeah, PAL. These are easy. This coulda been a two-fer night."

"Probably, but we have a mission."

"Mission! Yeah! A real mission. Consider that for a minute. Not just snaggin' a car for profit…for a run to an island to meet a mysterious lady."

"You're dramatising."

"No!"

"You're right. You're over-dramatising."

Malik took another sip of rum. More than a sip. He drank until it filled his mouth. He felt the tingling on his tongue as he held it, enjoyed it for a moment, let it slide to his stomach, and sucked in a deep, slow breath. The air was cool on his throat.

"Yeah. This night just doesn't feel real, does it?"

"It's real."

"How can you tell? Really? My new *360* virtual reality video and games mode could be bad news. Someone could have locked me in a virch and I might not know for hours. I could be just sitting at home and some shady CI has control of my gaming and video feeds and is running me through some crazy game. My full video is good, I'd never know it from reality."

"If it were a virch or video, I'd be able to see pixelation. I see none. This is real."

Malik took another sip of sweet rum, swallowed, bit his tongue, felt the sting of the bite, sighed, butterflies danced in his stomach.

"Reality, I guess. Any cars, PAL?"

"You have a couple of good choices."

Two of the cars highlighted in Malik's vision.

"Both skimmers, heat signatures suggest the owners went inside recently. We'll need to check the locks."

Malik walked to the nearest car, stopped behind and to one side.

"Can you see it?"

"Yeah. Deadbolt lock."

"Alarm?"

"Take a step closer."

Malik took out his pipe and held it in the light, close to his eyes, as he took a step closer to the car.

In Malik's vision, PAL-Malik showed red, swirling lines on the car, indicating electromagnetic activity all over its surface.

"360 alarm!"

"Damn! We gotta get a kit to break those." Malik sighed in frustration "We need a quick one. Thought we were gonna get lucky. Let's check the next one."

As he walked, Malik took out his tobacco. He stopped behind the car to fill his pipe and got the same results—360 alarm.

Malik walked to the edge of the parking lot and sat on the low stone wall running along the back. He searched all his pockets before finding matches. After a couple of hauls on the pipe, another car pulled into the parking lot. Two people got out and walked inside; both wore bandannas like Malik.

"YO, BANDITS!" they screamed as they walked into the pub.

"Not a chance on that Pacer, eh?"

"360 Alarm. Standard Equipment."

"What about the rest?"

"All cold. Everyone's been inside for a while and could come out anytime. These four are skimmers."

Four of the cars highlighted in Malik's vision.

"Let's check the first one." Malik walked to the nearest car.

"360 Alarm."

"Alright. Next one."

Malik took a haul on his pipe, enjoyed the taste of the smoke, and chased it with a gulp of rum. He stopped beside the next car, stoked his pipe, took a haul, and walked away when PAL-Malik found a 360 Alarm. The last two cars had the same results.

Malik walked to the back of the parking lot again, sat on the low stone wall, tapped out his pipe, and returned it to his pocket. All the while, the disappointment of not finding a car quickly built a lump in his throat, an empty feeling in his stomach, and pulled the ends of his lips down.

"Can't just sit here and wait."

"Look left," PAL-Malik messaged.

Malik turned his head.

"The next lot, the black Andalusian, those little cars always have easy locks. Ambient temperature, the building closed. Could be parked for the night."

"Let's check the alarm."

Malik began walking with renewed enthusiasm, the rush of adrenaline bringing some cheer, his lips arced up into a grin as he took a celebratory sip of rum. But upon finding another 360 alarm, the pain and pang of disappointment returned with a greater ferocity. Malik took out his flask and took another gulp of rum.

"We can't fail tonight. Usually, there's always tomorrow night, but—" Malik sighed, a deep, long, sad sigh, his frown returned, tears of disappointment filled the space behind his eyes and threatened to run down his cheeks.

"We might not be free tomorrow night. And this disguise…gonna look outta place tomorrow…how am I gonna hide my face? Let's try a walk down the street."

A couple of gulps of rum later, Malik saw a car park across the street. Someone got out and went into the building.

"Did you see the Breton parked across the street?"

"You bet. Check that place. What is it?" Malik silently messaged PAL-Malik.

"Art school, gallery…there's an exhibit tonight, all-nighter."

"He could be inside for a while."

"Could be."

Malik crossed the street quickly in the light traffic. The rush was back, he grinned at the new opportunity, his heart pounded as he approached the car.

Bah-boom…bah-boom…bah-boom…bah-boom.

"Just a little sip to cool the nerves."

Malik drained the flask. The last swallow filled his mouth with a comforting burn and taste.

"It's only got a door alarm. Deadbolt lock."

Malik swallowed. The rum burned its way to his stomach. He stopped beside the car door and tipped the flask to his lips again. As he did, he held his other hand beside the car door. A wire sprang out from his wristband and slid inside the space between the door and frame.

"Alarm is…dead. Lock…open. We're in."

The door opened and the wire recoiled back into Malik's wristband. There were four seats inside, all facing the centre. Malik jumped in the nearest one and closed the door. He held his wristband near the side beside the door. The wire sprang out again and slid inside the panels.
"Communicatiooooons…off…aaaannnnd…got it. We're on our way!" PAL-Malik messaged.
The car started moving.
"YEAH, BABY!" Malik slapped his fist into his palm. "YOOUU HOOOO HOOO."

With the car in motion, a euphoric wave washed over Malik. His rush of excitement grew as PAL-Malik drove the car onto the street. His skin tingled, his mind raced.
"Top o' the world, baby! WHOOOO!"
He tapped himself on the shoulder, remembered his flask, and tipped up a drink. "Nuthin'…stop, stop, stop, PAL. The store. I gotta get a bottle."

"Did you forget you're wanted for murder? You buy anything and the transaction will be flagged. The police will be here in minutes."

"Oh yeah. Mission for real. AND WE GOT THE CAR! YOOOOH! THERE! The guy, on the bench, with the bottle! Pull up beside him. Drop the window."

PAL-Malik slowed the car to a stop near the sidewalk bench. A Duarga sat there wearing bandannas, but the one covering his nose and mouth was pulled down around his neck, and the top one was pushed up to the top of his head. His pipe lay on the bench beside his leg. Malik took his tobacco out of his pocket and leaned out the open window holding his tobacco in one hand and his flask in the other.

"WOOO, BANDITS WIN! Hey, I'll give ya' a pinch o' backie for a swig o' whiskey!"

The Duarga picked up his pipe and got off the bench.

He staggered a couple of steps to the car, holding his pipe in one hand and a large bottle of whiskey in the other, slurring heavily as he said, "Ah'll fill yer flass if ya fill me pipe."

"Oh yeah!"

While Malik filled the Duarga's pipe, the Duarga failed miserably filling Malik's flask, spilling more than he filled.

"Lem-me, lemme, I'll do it. Ya gonna waste it all!" Malik said.

Malik handed the full pipe back to the Duarga and took the bottle. He lifted the bandanna over his mouth and chugged a couple of gulps, then filled the flask while the Duarga burnt his fingers trying to light his pipe.

"Wouldja…would ya mind, laddie?" He steadied himself with one hand while he offered the pipe and matches with the other. "Can't seem ta git me pipe goin'."

"Yeah, hahaha—" Malik laughed heartily. "Tough sometimes to get match and pipe in the same place."

Malik offered him the bottle as he reached for the pipe and matches.

"Take a swig first…take a—"

Malik tipped the bottle back and a delicious tingle filled his mouth. He gulped and swallowed.

"Take a good swaller—"

Malik gulped again. The crisp, clean flavour and tingle were a different experience from the sweet burn of the rum. The whiskey slid cleanly to the stomach, not like the trail burnt by the rum. Malik enjoyed two more delicious gulps of whiskey before handing back the bottle and lighting the Duarga's pipe.

After a fist bump, Malik screamed,

"YOOOH, BANDITS!"

The Duarga staggered back to his bench, puffing his pipe. He fell, then managed to get up enough to sit on the sidewalk in front of the bench. Instead of trying to climb back on the bench, he sat in front of it and used it as an elbow rest while he smoked.

"WAHOOOO…PAL-MAL…wherezz…ah…where to now? Are we…are we there yet?"

"Yes, this is the parking lot…aaannnnd…there are the trees."

Malik jumped out of the car as soon as it stopped. He ran behind the trees, where Allie, Sihanna, and Damien waited.

"Let's go! Let's…we got to go! No time to wait," Malik waved them on as he spoke and took a few deep breaths the air dried his mouth. He took a sip of whiskey, felt the comforting wetness in his mouth, swished it around, and swallowed. "Come on, this way."

Malik trotted back to the car, closely followed by Allie, Sihanna, and Damien. They all got in, Malik connected the wire again, PAL-Malik took control of the car, and they backed out of the parking lot.

"YEAH, BABY!" Malik clapped his hands twice, then lifted the bandanna over his mouth and took a gulp of whiskey.

"Mal, just get over the water, get away from the cameras…are you drunk?" Allie shook her head.

"Relax Allie, jus' had a couple o' sssips. Flas' was almos' empty. Yeah…YEAH! To the water! PAL-Mal, fffastest way to the water."

"On our way. I'll get the directions to the island from Damien."

"Sing it out loud, baby!" Malik clapped his hands and laughed. "Tell everyone where we're goin'."

"We are going west on Fox Street; we'll be at South Skimmer-Run in about five minutes. On South Skimmer-Run, we'll get up to skimmer speed, take off and be over the water less than a minute later. I will need directions, Damien."

"Twenty-six degrees east of due south for six hundred klicks. Wow, guess I know why Dad said that every time we went there."

"Hey, wha' ya get to eat?" The bite of hunger in Malik's empty stomach was quickly replaced with panic. "PAL-Mal, we got enough fuel for the jets?"

"We're good, about a hundred klicks to spare."

Allie handed him a red bandanna, tied at the four corners. Malik pulled the red bandanna around his nose and mouth down around his neck and pushed the white one to the top of his head. He put the bandanna from Allie in his lap and untied two of the corners. Inside was a mix of nuts, berries, and meal pods.

He grabbed some with his fingers, tilted his head back, and dropped them in his mouth. The sweet berries mixed with the nuts and the light spice of the meal pods created a glorious taste.

"Ooohhh, 'at's tasty."

Malik swallowed and dropped more into his mouth. His tongue was brushed with a new burst of flavour. He chewed quickly, swallowed, and dropped more in his mouth.

Allie grinned. "Want a shovel, Mal?"

Malik chewed a few times, swallowed and shook his head, "Starvin'."

He dropped another handful into his mouth.

Shortly, after turning off Fox Street, PAL-Malik announced, *"Hold on, accelerating to skimmer speed."*

Malik felt the car speed up as he finished his snack. Wings extended from the back near the top, and lower front near the wheels, jet engines swung out over the rear wheels and roared to life…the car slowly lifted off the stone-paved road and continued skimming over the surface using ground effect. The car had the power to climb higher and actually fly, but air traffic control laws limited cars to ground-effect flying. Cars had to stay close to the surface, using the cushion of air created between the surface and a moving vehicle to enable very low-altitude flight.

"We will be over the water in ten seconds."

As the land fell behind, Malik sighed and took a sip of whiskey. "No more cameras."

"Sooo…we can't be caught now?" Allie shrugged.

"As soon as the owner finds his car missing, he'll report it. Camera search will track us over the water, then they'll wait for us, or the car, to show up on a camera somewhere. So as long as a camera never sees us—" Malik shrugged his shoulders, "we're safe."

Allie shook her head. "So we have to stay in the wilderness?"

"Mira's living on an island, she's gotta have transportation," Damien shrugged.

"Yeah…how long till we get there?" Allie asked.

"About two hours twenty minutes," replied PAL-Malik.

Malik took another sip of whiskey. "Hey, I'm almost empty. Check the pockets—maybe there's a bottle."

They all checked the storage compartments in the door beside each seat.

"What's in here?" Malik lifted up the cover, peering inside 'Nothing.'

"Whose car did ya steal, Mal?" The tension and concern in Allie's voice was reflected in her face when Malik looked up.

"Wow! A 3MP24, nice gun," Damien said.

"Yeah! Lotta firepower. Not something many people have."

"Here's the mags." Sihanna handed the magazines to Allie who put two in her lap and slipped one into the grip.

She looked at Malik with a question.

"Yeah. My Peashooter can only shoot fives; this thing can fire tens. We mighta stopped those guys back there with this. The laser nade could have blown them in half. This is not someone's personal defence weapon, Mal. This is standard issue for Military Infantry. Whose car, Mal?"

"Ah, doone know, not a…not a good idea to stick around and…(hiccup)…and get a name in cases like this. Hey, lemme see." He reached for the gun.

"NO! You're wasted! You're not getting a gun."

"Just pull the mag out."

Allie pulled the magazine out and put it, the other two, and the gun on the floor between her and Sihanna's seats.

"Not wasted," Malik complained.

Allie gave Malik a wide-eyed, condescending stare, and nodded. "Uh-huh."

Malik leaned his head back. "Ahmmmm…thirsty." He took a gulp of whiskey, looked ahead again, and added, "So, nuthin' to drink?"

Damien sniffed a couple of times. "Is that whiskey? Thought you had rum?"

"Did. Gotta refill. Try, isssits good."

Damien took the flask. He took a sip, swallowed…and took another sip. He handed the flask back to Malik. "Yeah, that's good."

"Yeah, ya Mom woulda liked it. Your Ma…(hiccup)…Mom liked whiskey."

Malik took the flask and another gulp. He thought of Damien's mother and conjured her image. Butterflies danced in his stomach every time he thought of her.

"She was gorgeous, eh, PAL," he messaged silently.

"Yes, she was very attractive."

PAL-Malik played a short video. It showed Damien's mother, Aalya, in the backyard during summer, standing near a table, barefoot, with red shorts and a white t-shirt. Her long, wavy, dark red hair straddled her shoulders as she giggled and drank from a glass. Malik's stomach butterflies went into overdrive when he remembered a hug.

"Yeah. Too bad she didn't like you," Damien interrupted Malik's daydreaming.

"Uhhh—"

"Dad thought you were okay."

Malik's stomach dropped. He felt his lips drop into a deep frown, and tears welled behind his eyes. "She. Didn't. Like. Me."

"No…but…I guess she and Dad made sure we were…gonna be okay—" Tears started to roll down Damien's cheeks as his voice dropped to a whisper, "No matter what."

Sihanna got out of her seat and sat in Damien's lap, put her arms over his shoulders and around his neck, and pressed her cheek to his as Damien embraced her and let his tears flow. Allie got up and embraced them both.

"I can't believe she didn't like me," Malik mumbled sadly to himself.

Allie's face popped into Malik's vision, translucent, on the left side. "Mal. What are you doing? Get over here!" she messaged with the video.

"Hey! I'm hurtin' here."

"Day has lost both his parents, and you want attention over a schoolboy crush?"

"I'm not—" Malik sighed. "I crushed on her since I was—" a cartoon crying baby appeared in front of Allie, "and I just found out—"

Allie pulled her hand back as if to slap him, but she patted his chest, rubbed the spot over his heart, and said, "I know, Mal, I know."

She then gave him a hug and disappeared.

Yeah, Day's Dad was killed…right in front of us, Malik thought.

He felt sweat beading on his forehead, he took a deep breath and leaned his head back. Some nervousness caused his hands to shake, and sweat started to roll down his face. There was a tightness in his stomach like the muscles were squeezing, holding in pressure.

"I'm feeling a little dizzy, PAL."

"Yeah, I'm gonna sober you up. Med bots are removing alcohol and THC from your bloodstream."

"Why?"

"I'm detecting an alarming increase in your heartbeat, and you've started sweating and shaking for no apparent

reason. Recording data for when I can consult with a med lab."

The nervous shaking of his hands spread to his whole body. Sweat rolled freely down his face, back, and chest, soaking his shirt.

"Gonna...gonna shake out of the seat, everything...everything spinning...what's happening, PAL?"

"Just relax, you'll be okay...join the group hug. Slip off your wristband and leave it on the seat."

Malik panted, shallow quick breaths, vision blurred, then darkened, blackness, then blurred again. He panted between words.

"Day's dad killed...we're headed into who knows what shit now. What if...what if, next time...we all don't...don't make it?"

"Try to relax, you'll be okay...join the group hug."

The shaking and sweating were lessening. Malik took deep, gentle breaths and his vision began returning; not so dizzy now, no blackout. He took off his wristband and tried to stand, but felt too weak when he leaned ahead. He fell back in the seat again, took a few deep breaths, and tried to stand again.

He took a step, lost his strength and balance, and fell to his knees. But one step was enough. As he leaned in between Allie and Sihanna, the shaking and sweating returned. He saw Allie's face, covered in sweat, drops collecting on her chin, falling off. She was shaking too, or was he just shaking so much it looked like she was? He lay his head on her shoulder; overcome by a wave of dizziness, blackness filled his vision.

***

Light. Dim light. Malik opened his eyes, blinked, and looked around. Allie, Sihanna and Damien were sleeping in their reclining seats.

"Oh yeah. In the car. Going to the island."

"Feel better?" PAL-Malik messaged silently.

"Yeah. Are we there yet?"

"In about five minutes. I was about to wake you."

Allie, Sihanna and Damien began to stir. They opened their eyes, blinked and sat up.

"We'll be there soon," Malik said.

"Yeah." Allie pulled her jacket close, shivered, and leaned back in her seat.

"We're at the end of the fjord, coming down from skimmer speed. This could be bumpy," PAL-Malik said aloud.

The wheels dropped down and the car came down in shallow water. It had enough speed to coast to the beach and up onto a wide, grassy patch in front of a sheer cliff face. The car turned left and a footpath was lit up by the lights.

As the lights in the car shut off, everyone reached to turn on their wristbands.

Allie stopped, raised her hand, "Wait, let our eyes adjust."

Malik looked outside. "Everything is black, the trees, the ground...but look at the stars!"

Allie peered out the window. "Maybe we should wait for daylight...only a couple of hours."

"Yeah. I'd really like to be able to see where I'm stepping," Sihanna peered into the darkness.

"I can carry you, Si," Damien offered.

"And we have no idea where we're going, could be hard to find a cabin in the dark," Allie said.

"There!" Sihanna pointed. "There's a light."

Malik looked where Sihanna pointed. "Yeah, I see it."

Allie and Damien peered out the window. Both nodded.

"Okay," said Allie, and she pressed the handle to open the door.

They got out of the car. Malik felt weak as he tried to stand. He leaned back against the car; legs shaking. Darkness surrounded them.

"Can't even see the ground."

"I got it. My fly bot can see infrared. I'll link everyone," Sihanna said.

"I'm good," Allie said. "Military eyes, I can see full spectrum."

"Hey, Si, what about your feet?" Damien asked.

"It's alright, Day. It's soft forest floor like in the park. I'll be fine."

The walking was slow, but after a few minutes, they were in a small clearing with a log cabin. A candle lit the window on the left of the door. The window on the right was dark, as was the window in the door.

At the door, they stopped, Allie raised her hand to knock, stopped, and turned. "It's kinda late. Think we should wait for daylight?"

Just then, the door opened. A dark-skinned woman, about as tall as Sihanna, stood there, holding a candle. Her wavy white hair stopped at her graceful neck. She wore a black shirt and black trousers. Her feet were bare.

"I've been waiting," she said softly. "Come in. Quickly!"

They filed in.

Mira closed the door.

Chapter 3

Inside, Mira motioned for them to follow her down a flight of stone stairs. She closed doors at the top and bottom of the stairs. The room had a stone floor and bare stone walls. They sat at a table near the corner, to the right of the door they'd entered. There was another door on the opposite wall. Mira held Damien's hand in both of hers.

"I'm so sorry, to hear about your father. It's on every news feed. I know it wasn't you. We—" she took a deep breath, "you saw the video he made for you?"

Damien nodded. Mira patted his hand.

"Do any of you need anything? Something to eat or drink?"

"Nothing to eat, but a drink would be nice." Malik felt a little queasiness in his stomach and messaged PAL-Malik to do something about it.

Mira nodded, and stared blankly for a few seconds, "We'll have something in a minute."

"I could use a pair of shoes. I lost mine when we were being chased," Sihanna said.

"My PAL, Jenny, will fabricate you a pair. Let's see."

Sihanna turned on her chair and Mira stared at her feet for a few seconds. "Okay, I have your measurements. Just be a couple of hours."

Mira looked at Damien again, and spoke softly, "I spoke to…the Military—"

"But the video, Dad said—"

"I know, but I know who to trust. They've taken over the investigation."

"Why would the Military take over a murder investigation?" asked Damien.

"Your parents were Militia, they were assigned Military duty last year. Two CI they worked with went missing, data and research were stolen…it's possible to use that information to mount a bio attack. Your mother was a genetic engineer, your father a biosphere designer; so, they began investigating how their work might be used. Shortly after they started…your mother was attacked."

"But how do you know it was an attack? I thought it was a freak accident."

Mira raised her eyebrows, widening her eyes. "A little too unlikely. Not often a meteor hits a car."

"So…what did you find?"

"First…Damien, and Sihanna, you're both Militia. Allie, Military School is your Military assignment. I'm a Marshal and I have the authority to assign you Military duties, which I have to do because I'll be revealing classified information."

"All three of you have the rank of Sergeant, and security clearance *Confidential*. Malik, I'm recruiting you as a civilian advisor. You'll have the same security clearance as your friends and the rank of Honorary Sergeant. You have the same authority as Sergeant, except in combat, you have no combat authority."

"Alright, that's…ah…good," Malik said, a few butterflies danced in his stomach.

"I need you to agree that any classified information revealed will not be shared with anyone outside this room."

"I agree," Malik answered, butterflies dancing in his queasy stomach. He felt the hair on his arms stand up, and he silently messaged Allie, "Shit's too real."

"Yeah," she replied.

"Damien, this may be difficult for you," Mira said.

"I've seen ahh…Mom's video."

"Okay."

A video emitted from Mira's wristband and played in the middle of the table. It was short, showing Aalya's car view driving along the road. A rock appeared and hit the front power pack. The camera feed cut. Views from other cameras showed Aalya's car exploding.

"We were able to get an infrared image," Mira stopped the video and the view changed. "See, this streak, here?" She pointed to a blurry spot above and extending behind the rock. "Recorded in infrared. That's the heat trail from the bird bot carrying the rock, guiding it to hit your mother's car. The bot was visually camouflaged…the *meteor* was a rock from a beach on Misty Isles. We were able to keep this video from the public, and the fact that it was an attack."

The door on the opposite wall opened and a cart wheeled in, carrying a pitcher of brown liquid, six glasses and a tray of snacks. It stopped near Mira. She put everything on the table and the cart wheeled away.

As they filled their glasses, Mira continued, "We have no idea who's behind it. We know they're well-supplied, all the tech and resources they need. And they've got people everywhere. Military, Militia, police, civil management…we've caught a few, all organic bots that shut down and immediately rot as soon as they're caught, memories fried.

"That's what attacked you, not Humans, organic bots. The biggest question is why the murders? We can see no reason. If some kind of bio attack is being planned, any information they would need, such as animal and plant species and how they interact, is available from public sources."

Mira shook her head. "The missing CI, your parents, the stolen research, the link is Har Megiddon. They were all part of the same team. There's one left. A Duarga, Aurelianus Riothamus."

"Has anyone warned him? His life may be in danger," Allie eyes widened.

"That's been taken care of. And…Damien, the Military has your father's body. We'll have a chance to get back in the next few days and have a discreet funeral."

Damien nodded. "Thank you."

"After that, we'll get Aurelianus and go to Har Megiddon. Everything points there. *Maybe there we can learn something.* For now, we lay low and hope we learn something before we leave. The story being released to the public, and all non-involved authorities is that all of you were involved in a classified mission and no further details can be divulged at this time."

"Wow," Malik silently messaged PAL-Malik, "I dunno, it's all too insane. Shit like this doesn't happen. Sure, this is real, PAL? I'm not locked in a virch?"

"If it were a virch or video, I'd be able to see pixelation. I assure you, this is real."

"Couldn't you be fooled too?"

"I'd be able to see pixelation no matter what. I see none."

Malik took a gulp of his drink. The sweet, fruity liquid teased his tongue, woke his taste buds, and filled his mouth with delight. When he swallowed, the cool liquid calmed his throat and stomach.

"Good taste, but maybe, something a little stronger, eh, PAL," he messaged silently.

"Probably not a good idea now."

"Well, here goes," he spoke aloud. "Wow, we're going to Har Megiddon. We should celebrate. Rum? Whiskey?"

"Maybe we should wait until we get to the Kettle," Mira responded.

"The Kettle? There's one nearby?"

"Aurelianus is on Udara Seven, living in an apartment, above the Copper Kettle."

"We're going to…to Udara…Seven…the Copper Kettle…there—" Malik stammered.

Mira nodded.

Malik took another refreshing gulp, and silently messaged Damien, "Did you hear that? The first, the real, Copper Kettle."

An image of Damien's face appeared in Malik's view.

"Yeah. Never thought we'd get to see the original, eh?"

"Right now—" Mira continued—"we wait for dawn, then go to Misty Isles and stock up for the trip to Udara Seven."

***

A few hours later, they arrived near a market on Misty Isles and got out of Mira's car. The stolen car had been hidden near Mira's cabin.

"We should split up. Five of us might attract attention," Malik suggested.

"Police won't detain us but what if *someone else* spots us?" Sihanna directed her question at Mira.

"I don't think they'll try anything here. There's not many cameras here and the few that exist are not linked. It would be difficult for them to track us. This is probably where they're operating from, so I doubt they'll want to attract any attention by doing anything here. But keep your eyes open and let me know if you spot anything suspicious."

"Yeah," Damien said. "If you want to get away from authorities and need privacy, Misty Isles is the place to be, eh, Mal?"

"Yeah, this place is great. Good memories." Malik looked around the familiar open-air market.

"You've been here before?" Mira asked.

Malik nodded.

"Mal grew up here," Damien nodded.

Mira looked from Damien to Malik. "You must have had a delightful childhood."

"Can't complain. So, we getting guns, ammo—"

"I was thinking more like spices and flavours. We're going to be in space for a few weeks. The biocycler can keep us fed but we'll need to add something for taste. I sent you a list of some of the things we can take. Here, take these." Mira handed each of them some small, rectangular, coloured pieces of metal and a backpack. "These tokens are used for money here. Red is worth ten, blue twenty five and black one hundred."

Malik quickly pocketed his money and sent Mira a silent message. "These people tracking us, they're gonna guess we're coming here. Only place we can hope to hide out on this planet. Sure, they won't try anything? They shot Day's father in the middle of a parking lot. These people are not afraid to kill in public, and it's a lot easier to get away with murder or kidnapping here."

"They killed Kian at night, and they were in complete control of the area. Had all the cameras shut down, and you were the only witnesses," she replied silently, then said aloud, "We'll be safe here, every time our adversaries have attacked, it's a situation where there are few people and they can be in complete control of the situation."

"They followed you for a week waiting for the right moment to strike. Here at the market, too many people, and too many unknowns for them to strike. Stay close to each other, don't leave the market area, and keep your transmitters on."

Everyone seemed relieved and nodded.

"They followed us for a week?" Sihanna asked.

"Hey, you guys, go ahead, I'll go it alone," Malik said. "You can have some fun exploring the market. Try some of the fruit…and fish. Delicious."

Malik started to walk away.

"But shouldn't you—" Allie called after him.

"I'll catch up with you later." Malik picked up the pace and walked quickly along the stone road.

On the south side were a few buildings, on the north, the market. The Misty Isles South Market was a large, grassy area with tents. Farmers, fishers, and all manner of artisans offered their wares free from the total surveillance environment found in most of the galaxy. Customers wandered around between the tents, while some sat at the tables scattered about.

"Busy for an early morning," Malik observed.

"Yeah, usually wouldn't be this crowded until afternoon," PAL-Malik responded silently.

Most of the tents flew a flag with a picture or word indicating the wares sold. A few of the pictures provided more curiosity than information. Malik soon spotted the flag with a bottle pouring something into a glass and hurried to the drink tent. Inside, he grabbed a bottle of Lassie rum from one of the racks and started to leave.

"HEY! Ya gotta pay fer dat!"

"Ho, yeah. Right."

Malik reached into his pocket, took out his money, and picked out a red token.

He smiled as he handed it to the Duarga woman.

"Sorry. From the mainland, my PAL usually takes care of that."

"Yeah, yeah, same story from yaz all." She snatched the red token and handed him back a silver one.

"Nine? Nine for a bottle of rum? Was only six last month!"

"Price went up."

"That's a big jump."

"Supply and demand. Lots more customers lately, but I can only make so much rum." The Duarga woman smiled.

"How about a little—" As Malik reached for a small bottle of whiskey, the Duarga woman slapped his hand away. "Paws off da merchandise. Ya wunts it, ya pays fer it."

A Human woman entered and the Duarga woman greeted her new customer.

Malik turned to leave.

No way I'm payin' nine, he thought as he snagged the small bottle of whiskey, and slipped it under his jacket, holding it in place with his arm.

He walked around the rack and headed for the exit. The Duarga woman intercepted him at the end of the rack, reached under his jacket, took the bottle of whiskey with a knowing look, and jerked her head toward the exit.

Malik smiled and nodded, "Have a nice day, ma'am," and he left the tent.

Outside, Malik walked to the side of the tent, pulled the cork out of the bottle and tipped it up to take a gulp. The familiar taste spilt over his tongue as the delightful rum filled his mouth. Keeping the bottle up, he swallowed and bathed his tongue with another gulp, and then a third. He brought the bottle down, held the rum in his mouth, and enjoyed the flavour before swallowing. He sucked in a long, slow breath.

"Love that cool taste after a good burn."

He set the bottle on the grass, took out his pipe, filled it, and searched all his pockets before finding a match. He picked up the bottle, took a gulp, held it, swallowed, and took a good haul on the pipe. The smoke filled his mouth, its smoky taste mixing with the sweet aftertaste of the rum.

He inhaled deep and slow, tilted his head back, and blew the smoke into the air. He repeated, then stuck the pipe in his mouth, held it with his teeth, took his flask out of his pocket, filled it and returned it to his pocket. He looked at the clear, transparent bottle no label; the rum half gone. He corked the bottle and put it in his backpack.

"Alright, let's see if we can find—" Malik walked deeper into the field of tents, scanning the flags. "Probablyyyyyy." He spotted a flag with a rolling die. "Yeah, by the road."

He covered the distance to the gambling tent with a couple of sips of rum and a few hauls on the pipe. He tapped out his pipe on a stone near the entrance and went inside.

"Okay, what do we have? Three tables, Castle Conquest, Dice Poker and Let it Roll."

"Thirty seconds to roll, one spot's open, young fella. Could double yer money."

The Human roller juggled three dice as he winked and smiled at Malik. His thin moustache curled up with his bright red lips, set on a round sun-bronzed face. His close-cut salt n' pepper hair seemed to sparkle when hit by sunlight.

His denim overalls and white t-shirt covered a barrel-shaped body, the pants stopping about halfway between the knees and ankles that looked too small for his size. The five bettors, all bare-chested Human males wearing rubber overalls with attached boots, probably a fishing boat crew, looked bored with the waiting.

Through the open tent door, Malik saw a freighter roll to a stop across the street. *Is SeaWise Sam getting a delivery?* he turned for a better look.

"Ten seconds," shouted one of the bettors, and all five along with the roller counted down the seconds, "Seven…six…five…four—"

Malik put all his money on the square with a one.

"Three—"

"Maybe I shouldn't." His left hand started to reach for the money.

"Two—"

His right hand pulled his left back.

"One. Let it Roll!"

The roller stopped juggling and rolled the die in his right hand along the table. It stopped on the five. The roller matched the money on the five square and collected the rest.

Malik stared at the die until the roller picked it up and started juggling again. "Fifteen minutes to next roll! Fifteen minutes!"

"Can't believe we lost that roll."

"Did you bet everything?" PAL-Malik asked.

"Yep. All of it."

"You ahhh—"

"Hey, Sam's got a delivery. Let's go take a look." Malik rushed outside, crossed the road, and walked casually past SeaWise Sam's gun and ammunition shop.

"Freighter went round back."

Malik slowly filled his pipe as he walked along the low stone wall that served as a fence between Sam's and the abandoned building beside it. When he was back far enough to clearly see the freighter, he sat on the wall and lit his pipe.

Two people, a Duarga and a Human, both males, came out Sam's back door and went to the front of the freighter. One of them opened the door, reached inside, retrieved something, and both left, walking around the building on the opposite side, out toward the street. Malik looked around and walked to the freighter.

"Anything, PAL?"

"Nothing. No signals at all coming off this thing. No alarm, no camera, no tracker. Just an easy deadbolt lock."

"They probably went to get something to eat or drink."

"Could be."

"Let's see if it's worth it."

Malik walked to the back of the freighter, stopped, and puffed his pipe. As he smoked, he stood close to the door and held his wrist near the lock. A wire sprang out and slipped in the crack between the two cargo doors. He heard a click.

49

He looked around, felt a rush of excitement, and opened one of the doors a little. Inside, wooden boxes covered the floor. Two of the long boxes were labelled as containing heavy machine guns; another had ten pistols. Most were smaller boxes labelled as ammunition or grenades.

Malik whistled. "No cheap hunting guns. Definitely worth snaggin' this one." He looked around again. "Whaddya think, PAL? Got time to get away?" His heart raced, he took a quick haul on his pipe to steady his breathing.

"I can be over the water in less than a minute. No tracker, so they'll have to spot us visually. If I get a couple of minutes, we should be safely away."

"And if they went to eat, we could have an hour." Malik looked around again, and felt the adrenaline rush, his arm hairs stood up, his heart pounded, *bah-boom bah-boom.* "We could be back at Mira's place before they even know the freighter's missing."

"Could be."

Malik closed the door and walked back to the cab door. PAL-Malik opened the cab door and Malik got in. He looked through the windows, straining to see around the building.

"Alright, here goes."

His fingers quivered as he held his wristband beside the side panel, the wire popped out and slid inside the panel. After a few seconds, the freighter started moving, pulled onto the road, and headed for the nearby beach and skimmer-run. In less than a minute, they were over the water.

"PAL, link with Day," Malik said as he retrieved his bottle of rum from his backpack and took a sip.

"Allie is trying to link with you."

"Link us."

Allie's face appeared on the left side of Malik's vision. "Mal, where are you? We're leaving soon."

"I'm on my way. I'll meet you at the island."

"MAL! Whad ya do?"

"What happened?" Sihanna asked as her face appeared in Malik's vision.

"Mal's done something crazy again," Allie shook her head.

"Well, if he's on his way back, he must have stolen another car."

"I did not steal a car," Malik took another sip of rum.

"Then how are you headed back to the island?" Allie demanded.

"I snagged a freighter."

"MAL!" Allie held her hand on her mouth for a second, "Mal…(deep breath)…what?" Allie looked confused, did a double facepalm, took another deep breath and puffed her cheeks on exhale. "See you, when we get there." she cut the link.

"Allie seemed upset," PAL-Malik observed.

"Yeah, only cause she doesn't know what we got."

"Mira's trying to link with you."

"Link her."

Mira's face appeared. "Malik, when you get there, park the freighter out of sight. When we get there, I'll open the hangar doors and we can move it inside."

"Hangar? You have a hangar?"

"Yes, it's where I keep the *Raccoon*."

"Who's the *Raccoon*?"

"That's what I call my RavenHawk."

"Raven…you have a RavenHawk?"

"Yes, that's how we're getting to Udara Seven and Har Megiddon. We're not far behind you, we'll be there soon. See you then." Mira cut the link.

Excitedly, Malik took a gulp of rum. He held it in his mouth, swished it around, washed it over his tongue, enjoyed the flavour, and swallowed. "Link with Day."

"Don't be excited and happy."

"PAL, hundreds, no thousands of times we've flown RavenHawks in games. Now, we get to fly in one for real. How can I not be excited? Day's got to be excited too!"

"Did you forget? We're going because his parents were murdered."

"Oh yeah. I didn't forget," Malik lied.

Damien's face appeared in Malik's vision.

"Did you hear Mira? We're going to fly a RavenHawk."

Damien smiled and nodded. "Yeah, lookin' forward to that. What cargo's in the freighter?"

Malik smiled broadly. "Guns and ammo, including a couple o' heavies."

Damien smiled again. "Heavy machine guns? With ammo?"

Malik nodded excitedly. "With long bullets—"

"We gotta set up and fire a few rounds when we get back."

"Ohhoho, countin' on it." Malik took another sip of rum.

"Seein' ya soon," Damien's face disappeared.

When Malik arrived at the island, Mira's car was already there. The rock wall in front of the grassy patch had opened, revealing a hangar carved out of the rock. The RavenHawk, looking like an oversized, beached whale with wings on top, was parked inside, resting on its wide belly.

The hangar was wide enough for the wings to remain extended, ready for flight. The nose pointed to the exit and the ocean, the gangplank near the nose, on the underside, was down.

"Park inside, beside the wall," Mira messaged.

The freighter rolled slowly into the hangar and parked along the wall. Mira's car moved in and parked at an angle behind it.

Malik corked the rum, put the bottle back in his backpack, got out. He stared at the RavenHawk. Smiled. From the beach the colour looked black, the close up showed navy blue.

"Look at it PAL, a real RavenHawk … Did you see it change colour as we got closer … And we get to fly it."

He walked to the cargo doors at the back of the freighter, and opened both.

Allie stood near the front of the car; arms folded across her chest. "Malik. Please, explain how THIS—" she pointed to the freighter, "is keeping a low profile, not drawing attention to ourselves."

"The guards just left it…plenty of time to get away, and no one saw me."

"Hundreds of people saw you leave! Do you really believe no one is going to come looking for a load of guns?" Allie's face was getting red.

"Sam didn't take delivery. He won't have to pay and won't come looking."

"Who's supplying Sam? They're gonna just forget about a load of guns and ammo?"

Malik shrugged. "No one knows we're here and we're leaving in a couple o' days."

Sihanna and Damien had begun looking at the boxes.

"I'll take some of these." Sihanna opened a box of grenades and put some in her handbag.

"Sihanna! Not helping," Allie said in frustration.

"Smoke and flash grenades. These might come in handy."

Damien opened a long box and took out one of the heavy machine guns.

Allie closed her eyes, sighed and groaned in frustration. Damien flipped out the bipod and mounted the gun on top of the car. The table that had brought them drinks earlier rolled from behind the *Raccoon* and stopped in their midst.

"Let's load up the *Raccoon*," Mira said.

She took her backpack off and put it on the table. Damien, Sihanna, and Allie followed suit. Malik handed his to Allie.

"Kinda empty. What do you have in here?" She looked inside. "Just a bottle of rum?"

"Told ya he'd forget." Damien smiled slightly.

Sihanna smiled and nodded. "Knew it."

"MALIK. You're twenty five, the oldest of us…I swear, it's easier to babysit a five-year-old!"

Damien put a box of ammunition beside the gun, opened it, pulled out the belt of long bullets kept together with wires and inserted the end into the gun.

Allie groaned and put Malik's backpack on the table. It rolled back to the *Raccoon* and up the gangplank, followed by Mira. "Ahhh…and I defended you! No. This is his first time going to space, he's gonna take it seriously, I said. He's not gonna forget, I said."

PAL-Malik messaged silently, *"Allie seems upset. This is probably not a good time to tell her you lost all your money on a die roll."*

"100% agreement, PAL," Malik replied silently, then said to Allie, "Relax, Allie, we got time. I'll grab something before we leave."

Before Allie could respond, bullets from a machine gun burst ricocheted off the stone floor. A second burst quickly followed, hitting the car. They looked outside; three large, shiny, silver crab bots with weapons mounted on their backs were on the beach crawling toward the entrance. The middle one fired a third burst.

"We're under attack!" Malik grabbed the grip on the heavy machine gun Damien had put on top of the car and pulled the trigger, firing wildly.

As they ducked behind the car, Malik put his hand to his neck and fell to the stone floor. Blood oozed between his fingers.

"SIHANNA!" Allie screamed.

"Got it!"

She took a square white piece of cloth from her handbag. "Mal, I need to move your hand!"

She pulled his hand aside and slapped the med pack on his neck. It melded with his skin and sealed the wound. Malik's arm shot straight up, his hand made a fist, and then his arm fell limply to his side. Sihanna held her wristband on Malik's forehead.

"He's good. Unconscious, but alive," Sihanna's voice shook.

While Sihanna bandaged Malik, Allie took over the machine gun and Damien snatched a box of grenades from the freighter.

As Allie gripped the gun, her tactical display showed in her vision. She linked with the gun and activated her targeting system. She felt every hair standing at attention.

"Second time, I have to shoot for real. Lot more firepower this time." Her stomach flipped a few times. She felt a lot more nervous than in the parking lot last night. Her breath sounded like wind, and her heart pounded *bah-boom bah-boom bah-boom*. "I know how to use this gun. I've shot these before, I know what to do." her finger quivered as she wrapped it around the trigger.

"Keep me calm, PAL."

"You're doing fine, you don't need me. You've had all the training you need for this," PAL-Allie replied.

She marked all three bots as targets, braced the gun against her shoulder, spread her feet in a firm stance and fired. The powerful recoil pounded her shoulder, but she held the trigger and kept firing. The guided bullets hit each of the bots but ricocheted off their armour. She switched to the laser and turned it to full power.

She hit the ground under the middle bot's front legs. The explosion flipped the bot onto its back. A roar filled the hangar as Damien and Sihanna threw smoke grenades. White smoke with silver sparkles filled the air near the entrance. The shooting stopped.

Allie stopped firing and looked to her right. The *Raccoon* had dropped a hover skirt and lifted off the floor; slowly moving forward like a hovercraft, the table wheeled down the gangplank and fell off.

She got a message from Mira, "Get in."

"Damien!" Allie yelled.

"Got him."

Damien scooped up Malik and led the way up the gangplank.

In the cabin were two pairs of seats with a space in the middle. Mira was seated in the furthest chair on the left, a wire from her wristband plugged into the arm of her seat.

"Put Malik in there," she pointed.

A door slid open in the space between the seats and revealed a medical pod in a closet-sized room. Damien put Malik in the pod and took the seat beside Mira. Allie and Sihanna sat in the other pair.

"I'll link you to the *Raccoon's* sensors," Mira said.

Suddenly, Allie could see outside. The *Raccoon* was moving through the smoke and the view cleared. She saw the weapons icon light up and the turrets extracted from the hull, two in front, one on top and one on the bottom, and two at the back in the same arrangement.

Two Human men wearing long grey coats and wide-brimmed black hats walked along the beach toward the hangar. The crab bot Allie had flipped, had righted itself. Three quick shots from the *Raccoon's* laser cannon destroyed the crab bots. A fourth destroyed the two Human men.

"More of those organic bots." Mira shook her head. "No point trying to capture them."

Allie noted four dots in the sky and zoomed in. Four silver aircraft came into view. Their slim, sleek fuselage and small delta wings glinted in the sunlight as they turned toward the *Raccoon*.

She noted the distance and said aloud, "Four Silver Darts, range thirty eight thousand."

"Keep an eye on them," Mira responded.

"Missiles fired. Sixteen inbound."

"We can't wait for them. We're taking off. We'll use the water for a runway," Mira said calmly.

With a burst of power, the *Raccoon* accelerated.

"Can't we use the laser to shoot them down?" Damien suggested.

"Too far and too much atmospheric interference," Mira answered.

"No machine gun mod?"

"No."

"Mass cannon?"

"If I use the sandblaster, the atmosphere will melt the sand—" Mira shook her head, "and I'm not firing nukes on a planet…unless I have to."

Allie looked back. The thrust from the engines kicked up a lot of spray and their heat disrupted vision. She checked their speed. *Thirty-five We need one hundred ten for skimmer speed.*

Allie kept checking the missile's distance and the *Raccoon's* speed. After about ten seconds, the speed passed one hundred ten metres per second, the hover skirt retracted, and the *Raccoon* rose off the water.

"Missiles at twenty nine thousand," Allie said.

"Six seconds to flight speed," Mira stated.

Allie scanned the sky for more aircraft. "We must have ships in the air somewhere."

"I've contacted Command," Mira said. "Air support will be here in twenty minutes."

Allie watched their speed rise past one hundred seventy metres per second, and they began gaining altitude. The missiles followed.

"Missiles at nineteen thousand."

Mira nodded. "We can't shoot them down, but I got an idea."

Mira guided the *Raccoon* into a dive, pulled out just above the water, and climbed nearly vertically. The missiles followed the dive. When Mira pulled into a climb, all the thrust from the engines punched the water and created a wave. The missiles hit the wave before they had time to correct their trajectory, and exploded harmlessly in the water.

Mira was breathing hard as if she had just finished running, "Timing. It's all about timing."

"Silver Darts are turning to intercept. They're at forty one thousand," Allie said.

"They're trying to get in gun range," Mira shook her head.

"They can't shoot us down, can they?" Damien looked at Mira. "I mean, games have to be accurate when real ships are used, and me and Mal, we use RavenHawks a lot."

"We should be safe from their machine guns, but their laser cannon can cause enough damage to bring us down," Mira replied.

"Sooooo …what now?"

"We can go faster, but we need time to accelerate, and if we keep climbing, they can't go higher than eighteen thousand," Mira transmitted an animated picture showing the limitations.

Allie watched as the Silver Darts split up, two going left, two right. "They're trying to flank us."

Mira nodded. "Our engine's heat will interfere with a shot from behind—a flanking shot will get them away from it."

"They're at twenty nine thousand."

"They won't shoot until they're closer than ten thousand, but when they *can shoot, we can shoot*," Mira said defiantly.

Upward the *Raccoon* climbed, speed increasing.

"Range fifteen thousand. How high you gonna go?" Allie asked.

"Can't go back, they know where we are. I'll take us to orbit and we'll decide our next move there."

As the range closed to thirteen thousand metres, their speed exceeded the Silver Dart's and the *Raccoon* began to pull away. Everyone began breathing again. The *Raccoon's* nose tilted down and they flew horizontally for a few minutes to increase to full jet speed.

Allie watched the speed climb to fifteen hundred and then felt her back press against the seat as the *Raccoon* switched to rocket power and began climbing vertically again. She looked down and saw the land getting farther and farther away.

Allie felt Sihanna grab her hand; she kept looking at the view.

My first trip in space, she thought excitedly.

"Wow!" Sihanna messaged. "When do you think we'll see home again?"

They were high enough to see the curve of the planet.

Allie felt the butterflies in her stomach. "I don't know. But I'll bet everything will be different when we do."

About twenty minutes later, the *Raccoon* was in orbit.

Sihanna unbuckled the straps holding her to her seat.

"You ever been weightless before?" Mira asked.

"No. First time. But I gotta check on Mal."

Sihanna pushed herself out of her seat and bumped into the wall in front. She tried pushing herself to the door between the seats but just ended up with a knee on Allie's shoulder and her face on the *ceiling*.

"Wow, this is a lot harder than it looks in virch," she said.

Allie chuckled. "*Looks like fun. Too bad there's not enough room for us to join you.*"

After a few more attempts, she made it through the door. Less than a minute later, her hand reached out.

"Allie. Pull me in."

Allie pulled her out and helped her to her seat. Tears were building up around her eyes. They floated away as little balls when she tried to wipe them.

Her whispered words screamed in their hearts, "Mal's dead."

Chapter 4

Silence. Interrupted by Sihanna sobbing. Her tears building up in globs in her eyes.

"How?" Damien finally asked.

"The shot—" Sihanna kept sobbing as she spoke, "the bullet was…the bullet—"

Sihanna sobbed too much to speak.

She transmitted the report from the med pod. Allie saw it in her display.

Electromagnetic (EM) charge from the bullet, disabled PAL, med bots, and shut down organs. The brain deteriorated beyond retrieval before being placed in the medical pod.

Allie grabbed Sihanna's arm and pulled her in a hug. Sihanna was shaking and crying. Allie's own tears filled her eyes and felt strange growing in one spot. She put her arms around Sihanna, and held her head on her shoulder.

She silently messaged PAL-Allie, "Do something. Contact Athena."

"We're conversing now. You know it's not healthy to completely shut down your emotions."

"Forget healthy. I can't feel this now. I have to help Sihanna."

"I'm doing what I can. Supporting each other as you are, is the best option."

Damien got out of his seat, pushed himself to Allie and Sihanna, and embraced them both.

After a few minutes, Allie was able to control her sobbing. "Okay," she said as she took a deep, slow breath, "we have to decide what to do. Who do we need to contact?"

Damien wiped a tear that fell off his hand and drifted toward the air circulation vent. "He doesn't have any family here, and no one he stays in contact with. Just his kitten, but she should be fine for a few days. She can take care of herself."

"Okay. What about—" Allie's throat closed and her voice stopped as her tears overflowed her eyes.

She tried again, but still couldn't ask about Malik's funeral.

Damien took a deep breath, and looked at Mira, then Allie and Sihanna. "Do any of us need to go back to Lutetia now? Couldn't we just go to the Kettle, get Aurelianus, and then go on to Har Megiddon? If we could bury Mal by the Kettle—" Damien shook his head, "no place, he'd like better for his return to the cycle."

"What about your father?" Mira asked.

Damien looked at Mira. "If we can come back, and know why my parents died—" Damien nodded. "that'd be better."

Mira nodded. "Okay—" She looked at Allie and Sihanna. "Anyone you need to contact?"

"School," said Allie.

"Yeah, school," agreed Sihanna.

"They already know what they need to know," Mira said.

Allie looked at Sihanna, then Damien. "Ready?"

They nodded and hugged again. As the *Raccoon* began accelerating, Mira announced, "It's eleven days accelerating to the wormhole, we pass through, then, ten days slowing down to get to Udara Seven." She handed everyone a set of straps. "Put the braces around your legs and waist. Acceleration feels like gravity, but it's low. The braces give resistance to your muscle movements, save you from bumping your head." She pointed to curtains hanging from the ceiling. "You can pull the curtains for privacy."

She closed her curtain. Then Damien closed his.

Sihanna pulled the curtain across the gap between the two pairs of seats. "You know how to put these on?"

"Yeah. Strip below the waist, wrap the wide strap around your waist, and let the other six hang down around your legs. Your PAL can link as soon as you turn on the power, touch the black gem…it's made of live mass…it automatically forms a mesh around your legs. Makes walking in low gravity feel more normal."

After she wrapped the strap around her waist, Allie watched the hanging straps form a mesh around her legs. "Wow, these things work fast. Are you ready?"

"Yeah. You?"

"Yeah."

Before opening her curtain, Allie messaged Mira, "What do we do with Malik?"

"I have a body bag we can use. That will keep him until burial."

As they accelerated away from Lutetia a news feed was picked up, for most of the journey they would be out of position to pick up a signal.

Marshall Murray, commander of Lutetia Defense Force, addressed questions about Kian's murder, "The murder victim, and the people with him, were involved in a classified mission, and I can release no further details at this time."

Their identities and photos had been broadcast when they were wanted for murder, when asked for confirmation, he replied, "I cannot discuss the identity of anyone involved in a classified mission." When asked about the unusual act of the Military taking over a murder investigation he replied, "Because all involved were on a classified mission."

The interview was short and ended quickly. Nothing about the mysterious men was mentioned.

The trip was mostly boring. Some time was passed selecting new clothing, though the onboard fabricator only had enough resources to make two outfits each. The video and game library helped, and much time was spent sleeping. And thinking. Too many times Allie thought of the last time she spoke to Malik.

Each time, the thought was too painful…her last words were screamed, just because he was being Malik, doing exactly as she expected. Each time the thought came, she instead thought about Katie, Malik's kitten. Thinking about a little grey-striped kitten running around, and playing with a toy mouse, was a lot more fun than crying.

She also had too much time to think about how the two great pillars of her life, the Militia and the Military, could no longer be trusted. At least, she still had Sihanna.

One night, watching her sleep, Allie thought, *She's so beautiful. How did I ever attract her?*

Allie felt a nervous tickle in her stomach. She caressed Sihanna's face, gently tracing the outline of her cheek with her fingers, down her neck to her shoulder and arm, then up again to her neck and along her chest. Her fingers trembled each time they brushed over a burn scar, the light scar tissue contrasted sharply with Sihanna's dark skin.

One year old…so happy you were too young to remember the burns that gave you these. Already got too many painful memories. The same fire attack killed your parents, ten years living in a war zone.

Sihanna groaned softly, snuggled against Allie and put an arm around her while she continued to sleep peacefully. Allie returned her hug, kissed her gently on top of the head and drifted off to sleep.

They had many occasions to talk while cuddling under a blanket.

"The Military saved us, and the Militia raised us. Now…people we might know, or train with—" Allie felt Sihanna tighten her hug.

"I know. Now, we have to trust our lives to one person…at least, she's been helpful."

"Yeah." Allie sighed.

Remembering the past, she thought of Alesia, her home world. Her first memories were there. Living in the Militia barracks with lots of other war orphans. Many happy memories from that time, despite ten years of war. The evacuation and move to the Lutetia system was easy.

Everyone in her area had moved at once; her whole social group had moved with her. She pulled up a picture of her parents. She had been only two years old when they died and had no memories.

She looked at their smiling faces, their epicanthic eyes, grinned and thought, *I have their eyes, they will always be with me.*

"Allie?"

"Mmm?"

"How much do you think Mira knows about…everything?"

"A lot more than she's told us. And…our take off from Lutetia. Don't you think it's strange no one intercepted us?"

"Not really." Sihanna sighed.

"We blasted our way out of a hangar, fighters chased us, launched missiles that exploded in the water…a satellite HAD to see that!"

"You think so?"

Allie nodded vigorously. "Yeah, you can't launch a toy rocket without a public announcement lest the Military investigates…but we weren't questioned, intercepted and boarded, no communications, nothing."

"Well, Mira's a Marshall. I'm sure she knew—" Sihanna shrugged, "who to contact."

"Yeah, I guess. Can't wait to get to Udara, get a reliable, private connection, and get some more information about her." Allie thoughtfully stroked the fox embossed on her wristband, covered in white silk, with nine tails billowing behind. "But I think we can trust her. We met her because of that video. It's like Day's Dad used his dying breath to get his son to safety."

Food was plentiful, thanks to the biocycler, where wastes were mixed with minerals and converted back to a porridge-like mix by microorganisms. This could be eaten as is or left to set into a cake. The flavours and spices brought along made for a lot of experimenting with new tastes. But four people, in a closet-sized room, with only curtains for privacy, for twenty-one days…made for a round of cheers and applause when the *Raccoon* landed with its nose pointed to the black sky of the airless planet Udara Seven.

Everyone sat silently, staring at the vista. Monarch Habitat was before them, its great black dome filling their front view, fading into the distance to the left and right and up. Old Monarch, the first part built, made from tunnels cut into the mountain foothills, was directly in front of them. Around and behind them were dozens of landing pads; most had a ship docked. Behind the landing pads was a launch track, running along the plain to the hills beyond. A cylindrical ship sped up the mountainside part of the track, nearly ready for its launch into orbit.

"A tower will come along shortly," Mira announced.

"Do we need to worry about being identified here?" Allie asked.

Mira shook her head. "We're fine. Police, Militia, and Military have been informed we're on a classified mission. No one will detain us."

Dressed in her uniform, Mira wore black shoes, black trousers, a black waistcoat, a white blouse, and a black beret with white trim. On her left hip was a dagger with a translucent, blue sapphire blade, a short silver cross-guard stamped with three miniature sapphire daggers, and a leather-covered handle.

Mira nodded toward the door. "The tower's nearly in place," she said. A panel slid back beside the door, revealing a cache of small arms and daggers. "Pick a dagger."

"Okay, that's it, I have to ask if that's a real Defender's Dagger," Allie silently messaged PAL-Allie.

"I can confirm, that is a Defender's Dagger. And it's not polite to ask."

"Yeah, you're right."

Mira took the dagger off, and put it back on the wall, "This will probably draw too much attention." She picked a steel dagger and stuck it to her hip.

Do you think she saw me staring? Oh, I hope she didn't see me staring. Allie messaged Sihanna silently, "Did you notice I was staring at Mira's dagger?"

"Didn't notice. What knife should I take?"

"Daggers, Si, daggers...take the rondel...the round one."

"This? Looks like a skewer." Sihanna picked a dagger with a round *blade* and put it on her hip, the sheath stuck to her skirt.

"We'll need one more." Mira took another dagger and handed it to Sihanna. "Could you keep this in your handbag?"

Allie and Damien chose a dagger just as the ship's door slid back, revealing a car inside a large lift, doors open. They got in, the doors closed, the *Raccoon's* doors closed, the multi-seal airlock unsealed, and the lift dropped the car to the road.

As they rode toward Old Monarch, Allie looked back at the *Raccoon*, sitting on its tail, nose pointed to the black sky, its wings folded over the sides. A little sadness dropped in her stomach. *My first trip in space, gonna miss that little ship,* she thought, then smiled and leaned back in her chair.

"What about the trip from Alesia to Lutetia?" PAL-Allie asked silently.

"That doesn't count," Allie replied, silently. "It was a colony ship. Open-air environment, it was like living on a planet or a hab. The shuttle ride up, we were just strapped in our seats. Even when we looked out in space, it was like a video or a game." She smiled again. "The *Raccoon* is a small ship; space was right there on the other side of the wall. This was a real trip in space."

The car sped to a tunnel, slowed down for a swarm wall airlock, travelled a short distance through a tunnel inside, and stopped at another tunnel running off to the left. They got out and walked down the left tunnel, to the end of a lineup. At the front of the lineup was a wooden door, with the copper-coloured words, *Copper Kettle*, printed above.

For about half an hour they watched people in front of them try to open the door. It jammed, every time. Sometimes guests asked the Duarga man serving as security to open it.

When they were next to enter, Mira grinned at the Duarga. "Still haven't fixed the door?"

He chuckled. "We aim to be authentic."

When they entered the bar room, it was nearly full. Most of the stools at the bar were taken, and most of the tables were full. Some patrons were dancing as a band played lively, upbeat music.

"This way." PAL-Allie painted an arrow in Allie's vision, showing the location of a table.

Allie followed the arrow to a table with six chairs. As she sat, an icon appeared in her vision indicating food and drink menus.

Mira sat on Allie's right. "Order something if you wish. Aurelianus should be joining us soon. And ahhh…his nickname is Half Ton."

"Half Ton. Why do you think they call him Half Ton?" Sihanna silently messaged Allie.

Before she had a chance to answer, a huge Duarga pulled out the chair opposite Allie. His right hand placed a large wooden stein on the table.

He sat, took a liberal gulp from his stein, swallowed loudly, placed the stein on the table, nodded, smiled and said, "Well, hello dere. I'm Aurelianus, but mos' people calls me Half Ton."

"Iiiii think I see why they call him Half Ton," Sihanna messaged silently.

"It's from a race on his home world, Shylow." Damien replied, silently. "A Duarga that can run a quarter klick carrying a quarter tonne gets the honour of being called Quarter. Not many can do it. I'd be able to do only about half that, but Aurelianus did it, and was called Quarter. During the First War for Shylow, he ran across a battlefield carrying two wounded comrades. He was called Half Ton after that."

Half Ton was huge. Sitting, he was almost as tall as Allie. His shoulders were almost as wide as the bar table, hands were big enough to pick up a watermelon with one hand. An open red and black chequered shirt over a white t-shirt covered his barrel-sized chest; the sleeves rolled up to his elbows showed huge muscular arms.

His black, red-streaked, curly hair hung just below his shoulders. His beard, curly and coloured like his hair, dropped below his neck and framed a jovial, Santa Claus face.

He looked at Damien. "Your parents were good people. Some o' da best times o' me life wuz workin wid 'em. And uh, we're all set fer ya friend, jus' gotta pick out ya tree."

"Thank you," said Damien.

Aurelianus took another gulp, and looked at Mira. "Any updates?"

Mira shook her head. "Nothing really. Bound to be someone here. Have you noticed anything?"

Aurelianus shook his head. "Nope. Dey haven't come after me yet."

One of the robotic server arms, rolling along tracks on the ceiling, stopped at their table and dropped a plate of beans in front of Aurelianus. He grabbed the fork from the plate and ate for a minute before drinking again.

As Aurelianus ate, Allie messaged Sihanna and Damien, "Can you believe we're here? Think about it for a minute…it was here, this room…this is where…the first soldiers gathered…the first battles planned…it all started here."

"Yeah, lots of history here. Have you decided on a drink?" Sihanna asked aloud.

Damien was much more appreciative of the history of the Copper Kettle, "Yeah. Tables even look like they're in the same place. Bar, dance floor, and bandstand are, check these pics, almost a thousand years ago."

A few pictures appeared in Allie's view on the left. She looked at them, selected one, zoomed in, and compared to the present view. The similarity was uncanny.

A drink image appeared with a beep from Sihanna. "I ordered you one of these."

The drink was orange at the bottom, lighter at the top with ice, and half the glass was filled with fruit slices. "Hmmm…can I just get a stout?"

"Try this. It's delicious. You'll love it."

Drinks arrived quickly, Damien having something in a wooden stein, and Mira red wine.

Allie stared at her and Sihanna's fruit drink, "You know, Si—" she picked up the drink and looked closely. "Not sure about this one."

Sihanna pouted and folded her arms.

Allie's stomach churned as she brought the glass close to her nose and sniffed.

Sihanna excitedly, and silently, clapped. "I knew you'd love it."

"I haven't tried it yet."

As Allie sipped, Sihanna nodded excitedly. "Well…well? What do you think?"

"It's very fruity."

"And delicious?" Sihanna nodded excitedly, with a huge grin, and sipped her drink.

"Yes. Delicious."

"Okay, drink up, we have to go dance."

"How are you so perky? Did you start drinking an hour ago?" Allie chuckled.

"For nearly a month, we've been living. In. A. Closet. We just got out."

Aurelianus cleared his throat as the server arm placed a tray on the table with six shot glasses filled with a black drink.

"I wuz hopin' ye could indulge me in a Kettle tradition." He took one of the glasses and nodded to the group.

They each took a glass, leaving the last on the tray.

Aurelianus raised his glass and said, "To those who are memories," and drained his glass in one gulp.

After they had done the same and put their glasses back on the tray, Allie messaged Sihanna, "Si, the dagger in your handbag, put it on the tray."

Sihanna took the dagger out of her handbag and put it on the tray between the glasses. Mira reached inside her waistcoat and took something from the breast pocket of her blouse. She put a lock of hair on the tray. The server arm took the tray away.

Tears stung Allie's eyes. She blinked, tried to hold them back, and failed. She recognised the ceremony, a warrior's last drink but that was Malik's hair?

She looked at Mira. "Malik?"

Mira nodded, a trail of tears rolling down her cheeks. "He fell in battle."

The band began playing an upbeat dance song. Allie recalled Malik dancing wildly, this was a favourite. Damien was already headed for the dance floor. Sihanna put her handbag on the table and tied her hair in a ponytail on the way. Allie chugged a quick gulp, and Mira and Aurelianus followed her to the dance floor.

As she danced, Allie noticed two men sitting at a table nearby. Both were dressed in black trousers and shirts; long grey coats hung on the backs of their chairs. They both had long, thin, expressionless faces and were staring in her direction.

She messaged Sihanna, "Those two guys, dressed in black trousers and white shirts. You see them? Highlight them for her, PAL-Allie."

"Yeah. Hey Half Ton and Mira can *dance*," Sihanna replied.

"You've got remote access to your fly bot. Get a closer look at those guys in black."

"I think you're being paranoid."

"I'm gonna message Mira."

"Possible," Mira responded. "I'll try to find out who they are. Pretend you don't notice them."

After dancing, the discussion turned to leaving.

Aurelianus pointed to the ceiling with his thumb as he spoke. "Skolto's in orbit, ready to go any time."

Mira smiled. "Oh, thank you. That makes travel a lot more comfortable."

Allie messaged Sihanna and Damien, "Know who Skolto is?"

"Nope."

"No idea."

***

The next morning, Allie and Sihanna were shopping for a locket.

"Wasn't it marvellous to sleep in a bed last night?" Sihanna grinned.

"Yeah, better than a chair. But from here to Har Megiddon will be a lot more comfortable."

"What about this one?" Sihanna projected an image from her wristband over their hotel room table.

The locket was gold, with concentric circles on a diamond-shaped cover.

"Yeah."

"Or this one?"

Gold, oval, stamped with stars.

"Looks good. Get me that one," Allie said.

"Hmmmm…maybe, I should get the diamond. Orrrrrrrrr…You gonna use your chain?" Sihanna kept looking through pictures.

Allie pulled up the bare gold chain hanging around her neck.

"Yeah. Getting to Har Megiddon will be a lot more comfortable. Skolto is a lot bigger ship."

"Hmm…who?"

"Skolto…our ride to—"

"Yeah, yeah, I know. What about Skolto?"

"He's a Goldenrod." Allie projected an image of a golden cylindrical ship from her wristband. "Old. Construction date: year five of the Imperial Era. Sooo—"

"Nine hundred and forty-six years old," Sihanna calculated.

"Hab section, spin gravity, we'll have quarters, with a bed."

"I might actually like travelling like that." Sihanna smiled.

"One exploration mission, system U 264.1225 x 143.0125 x 43.3522."

Sihanna chuckled. "*Interesting name*."

"Catalogue name hasn't been settled. Retired to Caranarheim when the Currie destroyers took over scouting duties. Now travels the wormhole network offering transportation services."

"What about Mira?"

"Whoa, yeah," Allie said and projected some images from her wristband.

"MARSHALL Mira Thabiti. Highest rank in the Military, born on Lutetia, fought in the Foundation Wars…and…her Dagger…one of three! But for a Marshall, with three Daggers, there's not much info about her. A few other people have three Daggers, and there's dozens of games, videos, movies, re-enactments, lotsa news articles—" Allie shook her head. "But for Mira, there's only one virch game…the Battle of Beautiful Mountain, her first Dagger. Then—"

"Where'd she get the other Daggers?"

"One, during the Mirsinneen War and—" Allie paused, felt some butterflies fluttering about her stomach, and continued, "one at Alesia."

"Alesia? When? Where?"

"Presented during the Alesia Gaian Rain War. Details classified. That's all it says. Not even a date. Same thing with the Dagger she was presented with during the Mirsinneen War."

"Isn't that a little mysterious?"

"Not really. Hundreds of Daggers have been presented for classified missions. And the info doesn't get released until the Empire declassifies it."

"Hmmm—" Sihanna nodded and went back to looking at the lockets.

"What is more mysterious—" Allie continued, "is that, a Marshall is usually in command of a star system's defences, so usually, lotta news articles, interviews…not for Mira, only one short Military interview, after Beautiful Mountain. After that, she disappears from public record."

"Can you find anything with your Military access?"

"Not much, everything is classified. Promoted to Lieutenant during the battle, assigned to the Imperial Security Battalion and then, a mission to the other Beautiful Mountain star. The Beautiful Mountain system has two stars, she went to the other star for a diplomatic mission Established relations with a small colony there and—" Allie shook her head. "That's it. As far as history is concerned, Marshall Mira Thabiti has vanished."

Sihanna looked up. "Did you watch the interview?"

"Text only. Here." Allie enlarged one of the text files. Sihanna read the short file:

Lieutenant Thabiti, your comments on the heavy losses at Beautiful Mountain.

We learned a lot about assaulting a planet. Every life we lost will save ten on the next attack.

What will you do differently next time?

I'm sorry, I can't share any further details. I have to go.

"That's it? Not much of an interview."

"Wow." Allie grinned broadly, then said each syllable separately. "Si Han Na. You're actually interested in something historical?"

Sihanna grinned. "I'm not that bad at history—"

"Hmhm…ah…Si…I would trust you to hack a mega node, rip out my organs and replace them, you can mentally calculate the trajectory for the *Raccoon* to get here, but history, Si. You remember the first time we studied history together?"

Sihanna leaned back in her chair, folded her arms, rubbed her lips together, visibly ran her tongue along the inside of her cheek, and said, "Hmm…yes."

Allie grinned and blushed a little. "You said, 'History…stuff that happened a long time ago, right?' and then, you clapped because you got *that* history question right."

Very monotone, Sihanna replied, "I was right."

Allie felt the laughter building, pushing to get out. She tried to hold it back but couldn't.

"I ordered a teardrop locket. Stamped with hearts and flowers," Sihanna said and showed the picture.

Allie looked at the picture, teardrop-shaped, stamped with hearts and flowers. Her stomach kicked with jealously.

That's so much nicer than the one I ordered, she thought, then said, "Change mine."

"Can't. Already put in the order."

"Then put in a new order, I don't want the other locket."

"Another order? Hmmm—" Sihanna puckered her lips. "Not sure we have the time."

Jealousy ripped across Allie's stomach again. "Okay. I'll order it myself. Where'd you find it?"

"Hang on…okay…hold on…I've changed the order. We're both getting the teardrop locket stamped with hearts and flowers."

Allie gave Sihanna a hug. "Oh, I love you, I love you."

***

By early afternoon, they were inside the habitat dome, walking in the burial groove to the tree they had picked for Malik. Still in the body bag, Damien carried him in his arms as they walked single file. Allie, Sihanna, and Mira followed. Aurelianus, with a large bag tucked under his arm, trailed behind. They stopped at an apple tree.

Damien laid Malik on the ground. Aurelianus dropped one end of the bag to the ground. He untied the other end and took out four shovels, giving one each to Damien, Allie, Sihanna, and Mira. They began digging near the tree.

After an hour, the hole was big enough. Damien put down his shovel and pulled a strap to unseal the body bag. He opened it, took Malik out, and put him in the hole they had dug.

Allie thought about the last time she spoke to Malik.

Why did I yell at him? she thought. *I knew what he was gonna do.*

She messaged PAL-Allie silently, "I can't think about that, can you…get rid of the memory?"

"Could cause a lot of damage if I try to suppress memories."

"Okay, I'll think about Katie."

Malik's kitten. She showed up one evening when Malik was gathering supper from the meal bushes around his cabin. Shivering and afraid, she hid behind Malik's leg. PAL-Allie played the video for Allie and linked with Damien and Sihanna.

"A saucer of warm milk calmed her down. she just made herself at home, and stayed," Damien said.

"Remember, when she thought there were no more pods on the meal bush?" Sihanna smiled when she spoke.

Allie laughed. "Yeah. She caught four mice to share with us. She was so proud, came inside, excited, meowing, jumping around. Then, she brought them in, one at a time. Put them on the floor in front of us and pushed them toward us with her paw."

"Think, she believes Mal made mouse stew?" Sihanna chuckled.

"I don't know, but she enjoyed her stew that night. Happily running back and forth on the table between her saucer and Mal's bowl. Constantly looking up like she was asking him if it was good."

Damien chuckled for a minute, then stared serenely at Malik. He took Malik's pipe out of his pocket, filled it and placed it in Malik's hand.

"Allie."

She could only whisper, "Yeah."

She dropped her shovel and took off her backpack. Inside was the bottle of rum from Misty Isles. She stared at it for a minute.

Sorry, Mal…wish I could hug you one more time.

She pulled out the cork and took a gulp. The harsh taste covered her tongue and burnt her throat so much she coughed after swallowing.

"Ooogh. Don't know how he drank that stuff all the time."

Allie passed the bottle to Sihanna as Damien chuckled softly. "It's an acquired taste. He drank it because not many like it, so no one asks him to share his rum."

"Yeah. Mal would always share. Would cut his last bean in half if you asked him." Sihanna took a gulp and handed the bottle to Damien.

He drank a sip and put the bottle beside Malik.

Allie dropped the cork in beside the bottle. "His flask!"

"I have it," Damien answered.

He pulled it out of his hip pocket, shaking it, the rum inside audibly splashing around.

When Damien shook the flask, Allie noted the name *Angie* scratched into the bottom. "Same flask?"

Damien turned it over and looked at the name. "Yeah, he still has it. Five years." A tear ran down Damien's cheek.

"Remember? She gave it to Mal the night we all met. She was nice, too bad we never saw her again."

"Yeah, she was nice," Allie agreed.

Damien put the flask back in his pocket. "We'll celebrate again someday, and have a drink on Mal."

Allie felt her tears building again. "Celebrate? Could be a while before—" She started to sob and silently she messaged PAL-Allie, "Do something."

"I am."

"Do more."

"I can do a little more, but too much and you won't feel anything."

"I'd welcome that right now."

Sihanna took a pair of scissors out of her handbag and offered them to Damien. "You go first."

Damien took the scissors, knelt beside Malik, and cut off a lock of hair. He handed the scissors to Allie who did the same, followed by Sihanna. Damien pulled a locket out of his pants pocket. He opened it and put Malik's lock of hair inside.

Allie fiddled with her locket for a minute before opening it.

Teardrop-shaped with hearts for love and flowers for memory. Perfect pattern for a hair locket.

"It is very beautiful," PAL-Allie messaged silently.

"Too bad I was never able to get Mom and Dad's."

"That's regrettable."

"I have nothing from Alesia. Not even memories before the war."

"We gotta finish," Damien started pushing dirt back in the hole with his shovel.

Allie picked up her shovel. It felt heavy; the handle was cold. "I'm not feeling better," she messaged PAL-Allie silently.

"Considering the circumstances, that's to be expected."

No, no, Allie thought, then said aloud, "Not yet."

She dropped her shovel, bent down, and took the pipe from Malik's hand. "Match, anyone?"

Damien, Sihanna, and Mira shook their heads. Aurelianus offered a box. She lit the pipe and took a long haul. The smoke filled her mouth, its harsh, burnt taste numbed her tongue and irritated her throat. She couldn't stop the cough. She passed the pipe to Damien. He took a haul and passed it to Sihanna. She took a haul and passed it back to Allie.

Allie took the pipe. "I can't…I can't smoke anymore."

She looked at Damien, then Sihanna. Both shook their heads. She put the still-smoking pipe beside Malik and picked up her shovel again.

After the grave was covered, Allie sat cross-legged on the ground beside it. Sihanna sat on her left, resting her head against Allie's arm, and Damien sat on her right.

"Return to the cycle of life, Malik Meirleachmath. Return to the cycle of life," Allie said.

Damien and Sihanna mumbled the same.

As darkness approached, Damien stood up. "Let's get going." He looked at Mira, then back to Allie and Sihanna. "See if we can find out why everyone is getting killed."

Chapter 5

"Yeah. I'm gonna like travelling a lot more on this ship." Sihanna admired their quarters. The room had a bed and a separate bathroom, big comfy chair, and a small dining table. She opened a door beside the bed. "Oh, and a closet. Too bad we don't have many clothes to put in there."

Allie hugged Sihanna from behind, rested her chin on her head, and said, "Don't worry, Sweetie. Plenty of material and power, we can fab whatever you want."

"Damien is at the door," PAL-Allie messaged Allie.

"Just come in," Allie messaged Damien.

The door opened and Damien came in. "Looks like travelling is going to be a lot more comfortable this trip."

"Yeah." Sihanna laughed. "Can't lie. Not gonna miss the *Raccoon*."

Allie smiled. "I will…really. It was our first real trip in space; the trip from Alesia doesn't count. This time, we did it in traditional, cramped quarters style, barely enough fuel…and not just for a couple of nights, almost a whole month." Allie smiled broadly. "Yeah, the *Raccoon's* gonna have a special place in my memories."

Sihanna looked at Allie in horror. "You can visit anytime…docked at one of the ports at the aft end, coming with us."

"We had lots of fuel left, more than enough to take off and dock with Skolto," Damien said.

"Got a message from Skolto. Acceleration to start in ten minutes," PAL-Allie silently messaged.

"You get that message?" Allie asked.

Sihanna nodded. Damien said, "We better strap in."

"No need. Spin gravity, we shouldn't feel anything. A little bump maybe."

"Yeah. After being on the *Raccoon* for so long, I forgot. How long till we get there?"

"We have to go back to Lutetia, twelve days to get to that wormhole, then five days to the Har Megiddon wormhole, then, decelerate and cruise in the Har Megiddon habitat swarm and, depending on where Homarus habitat is in orbit, two or three more weeks."

"Wow. Over a month yet." Damien sighed.

Allie and Sihanna hugged Damien.

Allie rubbed the top of his bald head and saw a small cut. "You shaved?"

"Yeah. Med bots do a great job keeping the hair down, but it's nice to have the room to do an old-fashioned shave."

"But you cut yourself! Bend down. Let me see." Sihanna went to the bed and took a bottle from her handbag.

"I'm fine. Got plenty of med bots coursing through my blood, cut will heal in a day."

"Allie. Lift me up," Sihanna stood on her toes.

"Alright…alright, here." Damien went to the bed, sat down and bent his head forward.

Sihanna took the cap off the bottle and used the built-in brush to apply a clear gel to the cut.

"This is why you don't shave yourself. Just let your med bots and PAL do their jobs…I mean, let your med bots keep your head bald. You don't need to give them unnecessary work by cutting yourself shaving. This protein gel should heal that cut in a few hours."

"Thanks, Si."

***

A month later, they were cruising through the millions of habitats and computer nodes that made up Har Megiddon Dyson Swarm, still waiting for a customs cruiser rendezvous. Habitats stretched in all directions. Many were ring-shaped; these usually contained a biosphere, some were inhabited, some were kept as nature reserves, some as parks, and some held historical recreations.

Others were spherical, cone, or pyramid-shaped. These were mostly computer nodes. Some were used for storage, manufacturing and microgravity habitats. Scattered throughout were the balloon bots. These were very large, spherical, gas-filled bags that could move about by changing the magnetic field across their surface and interacting with the star's magnetic field. They were used to collect occasional orbital debris.

They could also use their mass to make orbital corrections needed by the habitats and aided in search and rescue when necessary. Looking toward the star, much of the light was blocked by a dense concentration of structures used for stellar husbandry. Some of the stars' heat and light were reflected back onto the star.

The temperature of the outer layers was raised and they expanded enough for the gasses to be collected and stored for later use. This slowly reduced the star's rate of fusion, extended its lifetime, and, eventually, would drain enough mass to prevent it from going supernova.

"Lot more ships coming and going here. Habitats extend deep into space. Lots of distance to cover." Mira chuckled. "This is where the legends of waiting months for a customs cruiser came from, and the games from that—"

Damien laughed. "Yeah, you wait so long for customs you start running out of supplies and have to survive until they arrive."

Sihanna had a look of horror on her face. "How close is that to reality?"

Damien groaned. "Ugh…Si, we can last for years."

She seemed relieved. "You're sure—"

"There's no worries, Honey," Mira responded reassuringly. "We can last indefinitely. And, according to the latest update, the cruiser should be here in a couple of days."

"But it was so quick and simple at Udara. All we had to do was broadcast our ID."

Mira nodded. "At Udara, it's all about the tourists. Gotta make it easy to get in and out."

During the cruise to Homarus habitat, much fun was spotting and identifying other ships. Most broadcast an ID, but finding out the type of ship by analysing the energy signature became a favourite pastime. All were too far away to see visually.

"What about this one? Still not broadcasting an ID." Allie projected the image from her wristband in the space between her and Sihanna.

Both were sitting on the bed in their quarters.

"Mmmm." Sihanna stared at the readings, "That energy signature is different, a long, thin line. Skolto have anything in the library?"

"Still checking…found this though, that really strange world ship from yesterday." Allie displayed an image of a ship, hundreds of hexagonal *shield* structures orbiting a brightly glowing, central fusion power source. "It's an Ice Cricket ship. When it's coasting like that the hull separates into pieces and orbits the central storage and fusion chamber. When they accelerate—" in the image all the separate hull pieces joined to form a smaller, solid hull around the reactor, "everything joins up. Separating helps with heat dissipation, Ice Crickets live in deep space, their bodies are made of ice."

"Damien is at the door."

"Yeah, come in."

Damien entered their room and grinned. "Just finished the Battle of Beautiful Mountain virch game. A physical virch, you don't just sit on a bed and let your PAL send video and sound. You're actually running around, live mass reforms into anything you need. It's not all images. It's great. Next-level gaming." Damien got more excited as he spoke.

"Fun?" Allie smiled.

"Yeah. A short battle, though. Never realised it before. Played as Mira. Lieutenant Mira."

Butterflies filled Allie's stomach. "Si. Let's go play."

Sihanna kept staring at different ships. "Nah, you go."

"Si Han A. How often are you going to get a chance to play a game, where one of the playable characters is someone we are—" Allie spread her arms wide. "Currently on a mission with."

"We both can't play as her at the same time."

Allie jumped off the bed, bear-hugged Sihanna, and dragged her off laughing. "Come on. You can play as Mira. I'll pick someone else."

"Okay, okay. I'll go. Shoes. I need shoes."

"Damien, come play again," Allie grinned.

"Yeah!"

The battle simulation was short, just four hours from orbital drop to victory. Afterwards, they stopped at the tiny pub aboard Skolto for a drink and food.

Allie chugged about half her stein of stout. The sweet, salty aroma filled her nose as she lifted the drink to her mouth and gulped, her mouth filled with delightfully familiar sweet and bitter flavour, the strong taste washed over her tongue, it slid down her throat, leaving a wonderful bitter aftertaste that turned to sweet delight with age.

She smiled at Sihanna as she set the stein back on the bar. "So much better than the fruity stuff. Was nice of Half Ton to stock the bar with some good drinks."

Sihanna grabbed a slice of lime from a bowl and dropped it into Allie's stein. She smiled as she lifted her glass of orange fruity drink, "Cheers."

Damien laughed hysterically. Allie quickly chugged the rest of her drink and ordered another.

Skolto's ID flashed in her view:

Identity: Skolto
Species: Cybernetic Intelligence (CI)
Persona: Duarga Male
Occupation: CI for Goldenrod hull LUT44, Captain, Imperial Defence Force (Militia)

Skolto's hologram avatar stood behind the bar, a male Duarga, a little taller than Damien, with a short, bushy black beard. He wore a red chequered shirt and overalls. His hand *guided* the server arm as it dropped another stein full of stout in front of Allie.

"Thank you, Skolto," Allie said as she set the stein on her side away from Sihanna.

Skolto's avatar smiled from his round, red, flushed face. "Can't have a thirsty passenger."

Sihanna grinned and took another sip of her drink. "How can we call that battle a victory? Eight hundred soldiers dropped onto the planet; only sixty-eight made it out alive."

"Cause we wiped out the battle bots the pirates had there, liberated the monastery, and Beautiful Mountain joined the Empire...and it was the first drop from orbit to attack a planet," Damien answered.

The door opened and Mira and Aurelianus entered.

"Customs cruiser has almost caught up to us. Should be alongside in an hour," Mira said.

"Jus' enough time ta eat," Aurelianus added as he pushed aside a chair and leaned on the bar.

Skolto's hand guided the server arm and he placed a tray with a bowl of stew and a stein in front of Aurelianus. "I'll have to adjust our trajectory. Some low thrust will be applied a few times over the next hour as we line up with the cruiser. You shouldn't feel anything."

Allie took another gulp and raised her stein in Aurelianus' direction. "Nice choice of beers, Half Ton."

"Hehehe…been sittin' here all day drinkin' da good stuff, have ya?"

"No, we just finished the Beautiful Mountain virch."

Aurelianus nodded as he raised his stein. "Good one. Who'd ya play?"

"I was Private Brake, Day was Corporal Skanes, and—" Allie paused briefly and felt the butterflies in her stomach as she realised she was about to say, "and Si played Mira."

Skolto had put a plate of meat and vegetables and a glass of white wine in front of Mira. She had taken her first bite. "Hmm, amazing what you can do with cycler food, Skolto."

"Sorry, Mira, didn't mean to bring up bad memories," Allie said.

Mira took a sip of wine and smiled slightly. "They're not my worst memories." She stabbed a morsel of meat with her fork.

"Well, at least, the good guys won." Sihanna raised her glass, drained it and got another.

Quietly, staring at her plate, Mira said quietly, "Not sure there are good guys in war. No one who fights is innocent. You're both from Alesia?"

Sihanna and Allie nodded.

"We were assigned to patrol a coast there. Scouts spotted an enemy patrol moving north, stopping at every small fishing town, and killing anyone who used cybernetics. Terrorists, Gaian Rain, they were called, organic supremacists. They believe only organic technology should be used and their belief system doesn't allow for individual choice."

"Anyone with a PAL or med bots was summarily killed. We moved south in boats stayed close to the shore. Came to…one of those small towns. Saw something strange on the beach, so we moved in to take a closer look. We saw twenty-two people, all Human males, impaled in a circle. When we got to the beach, we saw two girls in the middle of the circle. Both had their heads cut off and had been raped before being killed."

"The surviving townspeople came out of hiding when they saw we were friendlies. The impaled men had been the enemy patrol we were looking for…and the rapists. The girls were caught while everyone else hid…then, raped and murdered. Trying to force everyone else out of hiding…GR kept promising to stop and let the girls live if everyone surrendered."

"No one came out. Later, the soldiers were surprised by the townspeople, taken prisoner while they ate…and the townspeople gave them their version of justice. Organic supremacists…no med bots, no PAL…no chance of survival…took over an hour for some of them to die."

Allie felt weak and sick, tears were building, trying to push through her eyes. She leaned her elbows on the bar and her forehead on her palms. "Oh, that's…I can't imagine."

"I hope you never know the feeling."

"What did you do? The townspeople, they…that's a war crime."

"Only if you believe war has rules and law. We didn't include all the details in our report. Just took the bodies away, wished everyone a good day, and left."

"You believe in Armageddon Theory?" Allie felt some shock, a sinking feeling in her stomach.

"Without a taste of Armageddon, there's no reason for war to end. If the politicians who decide we go to war had to lead the army on the front lines, war would be obsolete."

Allie got a silent message from Sihanna, "What's Armageddon Theory?"

"War with no law, no rules of engagement, nothing is illegal. Theoretically, it makes war so terrible, no one is willing to fight."

"A RavenHawk from the customs cruiser Amboso is approaching and will dock soon," Skolto said. "Requested you meet 'em at the airlock."

"Amboso, another Goldenrod. Friend o' yours, Skolto?" Aurelianus asked.

"Amboso has met me here a few times. Been working as a customs cruiser since our forced retirement from scouting."

As they made their way to the airlock, Mira reminded them, "No worries about being ID'ed. Authorities have been informed we're on a classified mission."

A silver Human-form bot emerged from the airlock checked everyone's identification, and the cargo manifest, carefully noting how much mass was being brought into the system, including everyone's weight. A remote-controlled camera detached from the RavenHawk and flew around

Skolto, inspecting the cargo bolted onto the outer hull. The process took several hours.

Sihanna yawned while sipping her nightcap at the pub. "Almost bedtime. Why so long and detailed with the inspection?"

"They need to know precisely how much mass is going into the hab; they may need to prepare for mass transfers…taxes and security. This is the seat of the Imperial Court," Mira answered.

"Yeah, do you think we'll get time to visit Subete NoMichi Habitat?" Damien asked. "There are public tours. Might be fun."

Mira smiled and chuckled. *You want to see the court jesters live?*"

Sihanna and Allie giggled.

Damien smiled. "It's a great show on video."

Every star system sent an elected member to the Imperial Court, where they debated, discussed, and decided the future of the Imperial Concordant. Officially known as Imperial Courtiers, these representatives were often jokingly, or disparagingly, referred to as court jesters.

Five days later, they were on approach to Homarus Habitat, a giant ring three hundred and twenty kilometres in diameter and one hundred wide. It spun slowly, producing spin gravity on the inner surface. The usually empty space in the middle of the ring was filled with a mirror array, reflecting sunlight onto the inhabited inner surface.

For half the day, sunlight was reflected on half the ring while the other half experienced night, the roles reversed for the next half of the day. On the daylight side, the green and blue landscape could be seen through the transparent roof that held in the atmosphere. In the centre of the mirror array was the docking hub. Everyone gathered in the pub for morning tea and to watch the approach.

"The docking hub doesn't spin, so if we dock with the hab, I'll have to stop spinning and there will be no gravity," Skolto explained. "Or we can take up a co-orbital position alongside and you can use the *Raccoon* to transfer to the hab. I leave the choice up to my passengers."

Butterflies danced nervously in Allie's stomach, but her excitement buried it. "If we dock, no gravity. And with lots of space?" She grinned with anticipation. "Sounds like a lot of fun."

Damien chuckled. "Ooo, can you imagine the virch room? Skolto, do you have any no gravity virch games?"

"A hundred and ten."

"Oh, let's dock." Damien nodded excitedly.

Sihanna nodded and agreed, "Yeah, that'll be fun. Let's dock."

Mira and Aurelianus both chuckled and agreed to dock.

After a day of enjoying no gravity games, everyone left Skolto, took the train to the ring surface, and gathered in Mira's hotel room for a supper of real food. "I thought we should meet here, more privacy than a pub. We need to discuss what to do next."

"Yeah, where do we start?" Damien asked. "What are we looking for?"

"Well, there's our biggest problem. I have no idea what we're looking for," Mira replied.

Aurelianus added, "Hmmpf, our only plan really is ta sit round and wait fer dem ta come after me. They've killed everyone else working on this hab's biosphere. I mus' be next."

"Jenny will link with Gammarus, the hab's Cybernetic Intelligence administrator to see if anything unusual has happened. Then spend the night exploring hab cyberspace. Maybe some of the other CI have encountered something out of the ordinary," said Mira.

"Athena can help with that," Sihanna said.

PAL-Allie messaged Allie, "*I can help with that. I'd enjoy a night exploring after a couple of months with no network connection.*"

"PAL-Allie can help too."

"PAL-Damien has also volunteered."

"Be a party o' five, PAL-Aurelianus wants to go."

Mira smiled. "Great, more eyes looking will make the finding easier."

The PALs spent the night visiting media and archive nodes searching for anomalous data. Some of the locations were more social and many conversations were had with other CI in the hab cyberspace. The next morning, however, results were few.

"What about this heat surge?" Sihanna pointed to an unexplained heat source detected in a lake a few months earlier. "Investigation found magnesium oxide on the lakebed. A lot of insect fluctuations."

"Nothing out of the ordinary, the insect fluctuations anyway. Not sure about that magnesium oxide," Aurelianus noted.

Mira sighed and sipped her tea. "How did the magnesium oxide get there?"

"Wasn't determined. Pure, no isotope trace," Sihanna said.

"That mouse excess in the west forest is a little high. No cause determined. Marked for further observation…still increasing. Should look at that," Aurelianus said.

Mira nodded. "We can stop at the lake on the way."

Sihanna smiled, almost squealing with excitement. "We can have a picnic."

"Sounds like fun. I guess we'll fit in like tourists for a while." Mira smiled.

A few hours later, Allie was at the lakeside. After helping Sihanna spread a blanket, she looked across the meadow on this side of the lake. Trees covered the shore on the other side. She was standing on the inside of a giant ring; in the distance, the landscape rose like a bowl. The whole width of the ring could be seen rising above that.

The huge habitat contained a natural open-air environment with forests, meadows, lakes, rivers, and towns. All were visible in the distant landscape. The atmosphere, high enough to scatter light and provide a blue sky, was held in by a transparent membrane; acting as a ceiling, stretched from one side of the ring to the other, held aloft on the sides by a high wall and the atmospheric pressure pushing it against the vacuum of space.

The two-layer membrane had water between the layers, its weight helping hold in the atmosphere as well as providing protection against radiation. The transparent ceiling allowed the more distant parts of the ring to be seen.

The green and blue landscape contrasted sharply with the dark grey of the night side. As she looked farther up, toward the halfway point along the ring, her view was blocked by the mirror array and none of the *top* half was visible.

Mira collected samples from the small crab bot she had released into the lake. Data the bot had collected was displayed in an image projected above its back.

"We can do more testing later, but—" She shook her head. "Nothing new from these initial readings. Everything was already scanned thoroughly. Not likely we'll find anything. No recording of anything going into the lake…just a massive heat buildup…and magnesium oxide residue…I guess someone just dumped some magnesium which reacted with the water to produce the heat detected…probably, smuggled in and they wanted to avoid taxes."

Aurelianus scratched his beard. "Sounds like as good a reason as any…water looks warm."

Aurelianus had worn short pants and sandals, and he walked into the water up to his knees. Mira ceased her pondering and stared at him.

"Okay, we're ready!" Sihanna yelled.

Allie stepped back to the blanket and sat. Damien and Sihanna were already sitting. Mira was just standing, staring, as Aurelianus waded ashore.

As they sat, PAL-Allie messaged Allie, *"Mira looks troubled."*

Allie looked at her face. Mira looked confused while she stared at Aurelianus. "Mira?"

"Ohh…ahh…yes, a nice simple explanation, but some of the magnesium could have been used to pay the tax. Seems wasteful to just dump it."

"Maybe there's a fine because it was smuggled," Aurelianus said.

Mira looked at Aurelianus thoughtfully for a moment. "Yes…you're probably right." Then, she looked at the blanket. "Sihanna, it looks wonderful."

A selection of sandwiches covered one plate, and another had cheese cubes, fruit, and nuts, with a bottle of red wine beside each.

As they ate they watched a few ducks wading in the lake. Bright metallic colours flashed on their wings and backs, mesmerising mixtures of blue, green, and red shades mixed with black.

"Your mom's work, Damien," Aurelianus pointed. She tweaked their genome to show random patterns. But that's not the most interesting part. Aurelianus picked up a cube of cheese and ate before he continued, "After they lay their eggs, they incubate for three weeks. During that time, they keep laying small, infertile eggs away from the nest to distract the egg thieves. Keeps predation on the nest down and more of the eggs hatch."

Damien chuckled. "Maybe that's why we had colourful pet ducks so often. I thought she just liked the eggs."

After eating, they travelled to the west forest. Their car was parked and they walked among the trees. The trees were not dense and there were numerous clearings. Several small groups of people and bots were walking about, some sitting to eat or drink. Aurelianus wandered off to talk to some of them.

As he rejoined the group, he said, "Mouse mystery solved. There's a group o' Gaian Naturists camping out here, temporary lodging as they immigrate and wait for transfer to their hab. They've filled the forest with tubers and undergrowth vegetables. Gammarus should have had data on that."

Mira shrugged her shoulders, sighed "Well. I guess we head back."

After arriving back at their hotel, Allie and Sihanna sat on their bed, about to remove their shoes, when there was a rumbling from outside, and the building vibrated. They ran outside to see a building down the street had collapsed.

Allie looked at Sihanna. "I think…that might be—"

Sihanna nodded and finished her sentence, "Yeah…that's definitely something out of the ordinary."

Damien, Mira and Aurelianus came running outside.

As they started running toward the collapsed building, Mira called them back, "Wait…wait…walk, I'll contact emergency services and make sure we have access when we get there."

A great deal of dust had been blown out and was now filling the street. Local Militia had already deployed; two Humans, a male and female, each wearing a mask and a black vest with a red X, held them up as they approached. Emergency crab bots of various sizes were already onsite. Mira and the woman stared blankly for a minute. Then the woman lifted her mask and rested it on top of her head.

The woman nodded, smiled broadly, took five masks from her side bag, and handed them to Mira. "As soon as the bots declare it safe, Marshall Thabiti."

"Thank you, Corporal Jones. What was in the building?"

"Nothing, it was empty. Not even powered."

Mira handed out the masks. They covered the whole face from chin to eyebrows and back to the ears, melding with the flesh to form a seal, with a transparent section over the eyes.

Allie watched the dust billow around her; already it looked to be settling. An icon flashed in her sight, indicating a file had been received from Mira—the floor plans of the building. She opened it. Small building, two stories, twelve rooms per floor, carbon iron reinforced stone construction. Maximum weight, various measurements and tolerances were listed.

"This could take a while," Mira stated.

"Yep, da cafe by da hotel got good stew. We can eat while we wait," Aurelianus suggested.

The night passed and mid-morning arrived before they could visit the building. The bots had cleared most of the rubble. Only a few intact pieces of wall remained standing, some of the larger pieces of collapsed floors and walls scattered about. Sihanna's fly bot flew about as they wandered around the ruins.

"Some of the stone looks melted…one iron piece looks…melted or cut through…residual magnetic fields?" Mira observed.

Sihanna shook her head. Looking around, she said, "The bots cleaned it up quick."

"Maybe they had help—" Mira looked at the building specs displayed in front of her. "Look at the mass of the building, the amount left, and the debris removed…there's over a thousand tonnes missing."

"Ground to dust during the collapse?" Damien asked.

Mira shook her head, "Almost half the building?" She sighed, folded her arms across her chest, and said, "Missing. Not here, so it had to be moved. And if there's that much mass moving about, Gammarus can track it. Let's see what we can find out."

Chapter 6

Mira was visibly breathless with excitement and started walking faster. "The hab spins, the spin pushes us against the floor of the hab, the floor holds us in and creates the illusion of gravity. Small amounts of mass, like people walking around, not a problem...but a thousand tonnes moving around is too much in one place."

"Gammarus will have to move mass to compensate and keep the spin true, or the ring will start to wobble back and forth, the ground will look tilted sometimes, water will start flowing out of the lakes and rivers...wherever the compensating mass is moved, the missing mass will be on the other side. Let's head back to the hotel. I'll contact Gammarus."

While waiting for an answer, lunch on a patio at one of the restaurants was enjoyed.

"We should go swimming. Be hours before Gammarus can let us know anything; we've got the whole afternoon," Sihanna suggested.

Damien shook his head. "Hmm, um," he mumbled as he finished chewing. "Swimming. Duarga don't float so good, remember? We tend to sink to the bottom when we try to swim." He picked another meal bush pod from his plate and held it up. "Good selection of roasted saur here—" he said as he popped it into his mouth, "delicious."

Sihanna looked at Allie. "Allie?"

Allie was still savouring the sweet potato from lunch, the aftertaste teasing her tongue with the pleasant taste of sweet starch. An image of Sihanna in a swimsuit flashed in her mind.

She felt her lips curl up into a smile. "Yeah, sounds like fun."

She opened her picture file and flipped through pictures of Sihanna as she finished drinking her juice.

In the evening, after finishing supper, Mira gave an update. "Well—" she leaned an elbow on the table, rubbed her forehead, and sighed. "There was a heat surge detected before the collapse…emergency response had already been alerted. After…it's like the mass scattered…just…spread itself out. Not going to be easy to track it."

"Live mass could do that," Sihanna observed.

"Yes, it could, but this was dead rock and iron…of course, a swarm bot could cut it out, and then split into pieces and scatter."

"*Wouldn't there have to be a lot of extra mass there before the collapse*? The bot would have to be big to move a thousand tonnes," Allie asked.

"Gammarus is still checking the logs. Maybe tomorrow morning, we'll know more."

***

In their room later, Sihanna was sprawled on the bed. She giggled. "We should go swimming more often."

Allie felt her cheeks blush, her skin tingle, and her smile grow from memories of the afternoon.

"Let's go dancing. We've got the whole night. Day might come," Sihanna giggled.

"Yeah, it's been a while."

"Day." Sihanna linked Allie to their conversation. "We're going dancing. Wanna come?"

"Yeah. Where?"

"Don't know. Meet us here as soon as you're ready and we'll just go explore."

Sihanna opened the closet door.

"Wow, you filled that fast," Allie said.

"Yeah. Spent a few hours ordering last night after you fell asleep. What are you going to wear?"

Allie looked down at her clothing. White blouse, black cotton shorts, white socks, and black canvas shoes. "What's wrong with this?"

"Nothing…but…this skirt," Sihanna pulled a red skirt out, "would look great on you. It's a bit too long for me."

She held the skirt against Allie's waist.

"Kinda short for me."

Sihanna smiled. "Nah, it's perfect. Try it on."

Allie slipped off her pants and pulled the skirt on. "Yeah. Way too short."

"Hmmm…spin around…no, it's perfect."

Allie took a few steps. "We're going out, my underwear will show when I dance."

"I know." Sihanna giggled. "I love those dancers' legs. You look amazing…oh, please. Wear it," Sihanna pleaded, then pouted with her bottom lip.

Allie folded her arms across her chest, stared at Sihanna defiantly, and thought, *Not this time. I'm not giving in. Give me strength, PAL.*

"Your bloodstream is about to be flooded with oxytocin. You can stop it yourself if you stay calm…but, of course, you secretly enjoy it when she teases you like this."

"But I can't let her win every time!"

"She's not winning anything if it's something you enjoy."

"Alright, alright…What are you going to wear?"

Sihanna jumped excitedly and hugged Allie. "Oh, I knew you'd wear it! You look fantastic."

"You looked great in that skimpy black dress last month. Did you get one of those?"

"Yeah." Sihanna pulled a little black dress from the closet. "But we're not going anywhere…hmmm."

"What about that pink outfit?"

Sihanna put the black dress back and took out a pink one. "I like the colour, but it doesn't look good with my skin tone…and I like having dark skin—" She put the pink skirt back. "What about this?" She took out a dark red skirt and blouse.

"Try it on."

As Allie watched Sihanna take off her tartan skirt and white blouse she grinned and said, "Yeah, I like that dark skin too. Show some more."

Sihanna giggled as she dropped her clothes to the floor and put on the red skirt and blouse. The skirt was midway between her knees and hips, the blouse was open over her chest, with three buttons below.

She spun around a couple of times, looked in the mirror, and said, "The blouse is a little too revealing in front."

"No," Allie disagreed.

"Guess I could pin it up." She pulled the blouse together.

"No. If I'm wearing this skirt, you're wearing that blouse. No pin."

Sihanna looked at herself in the mirror and sighed.

"I could get changed." Allie grinned and thought, *I might win this one.*

"No...no...okay, I'll wear this...no pin."

Gotcha! Allie thought, chuckled and hugged Sihanna.

"And I got you the perfect dancing shoes," Sihanna said excitedly. She went back to the closet and pulled a pair of black, strap, low heel shoes off a shelf. "You can't wear socks with these."

Allie sat on the bed took off her shoes and socks and put on her new dancing shoes. She stood and took a few steps.

"Spin around," Sihanna grinned and blushed.

Allie spun a couple of times and Sihanna giggled. "You're right, your underwear will show when you dance." She giggled again and straightened the collar on Allie's blouse, one hand on each side.

Allie felt her skin tingle, her heart racing, her breath short and quick. She put her hands to Sihanna's cheeks, her fingers nervously brushing back to her hair, her thumbs gently caressing her cheeks. Sihanna tilted her head back slightly, Allie moved her fingers down to the back of Sihanna's neck and her thumbs tickled her throat. When she leaned close she felt Sihanna's hands leave her collar and her fingers softly stroke her neck before combing through her hair.

"Damien is at the door," PAL-Allie messaged.

Nooooo! Allie thought, then said, "Tell him to come in."

At the same time, she got a message from Sihanna, "Ten minutes…no, twenty."

Damien entered wearing his usual jeans and t-shirt. "Wow. Special occasion?"

"Yes," Sihanna answered. "First time we've gone dancing in months."

"What about at the Kettle? That was…oh…yeah, over a month ago. Wow, time flies."

"And we were dancing for…ten minutes?" Sihanna shrugged and shook her head.

"Yeah, I guess. You ready to go?" Damien asked.

"Yeah, let's get going, we can do our faces on the way. You should highlight your cheeks a little more," Sihanna suggested.

Damien looked at his face in the mirror. "You think?"

"Yeah. Link with Athena. She'll fix you up."

They walked out into the warm evening air, looking in both directions down the street.

Allie checked her map. "There's a dance hall about a ten minute walk that way. Nonstop music."

"Sounds like our place," Sihanna grinned excitedly.

"Okay, PAL, fix my face," Allie messaged PAL-Allie.

"What do you want done?"

A list appeared in Allie's vision. "I don't know. Contact Athena, and see what Sihanna wants."

The walk was short. The dance hall was a single-story, stone brick building painted with random bright, glowing colours. The dark bare stone showed through in some places. Inside there was a short hallway down the middle with a door at the end and two others across from each other about halfway. Music blared from all three doors. The door at the end had a sign reading: All Dance All Day.

"That's the one we want." Sihanna hurried down the hallway and into the dance hall. She didn't wait to find a table or order a drink, just headed straight for the half-filled dance floor.

"Wow, she really wanted to get out," Damien said.

"Yeah. You know how she loves to dance. And it's not too crowded here. Let's get a table." Allie looked for a table near the dance floor, spotted one, nudged Damien, and ordered a drink as she walked to it. A server arm dropped from the ceiling and put a stein in front of her when she sat.

"Day, you check the drink list? They have that strong stuff you like."

Damien smiled. "Rocket Fuel?"

"Yeah."

Allie got a message from Sihanna, Damien was also tagged. "Where are you?"

"Getting a table…and a drink. You want something?"

"Haven't decided yet. Come dance."

A server arm dropped a half-filled, short, clear glass in front of Damien. He picked it up, swished it around, smelled it, took a sip, licked his lips, nodded, and then drained the glass. By the time he placed the empty glass on the table, a server arm had dropped another full one. It collected the empty glass and retracted to the ceiling.

"Let's go dance with Si," he said.

A few butterflies tickled in Allie's stomach when she stood and started walking.

"This skirt is way too short Si," she messaged.

"But you look amazing!"

Allie grinned and felt her stomach tighten. She buried her nervousness with a few quick steps and began dancing toward Sihanna, who squealed excitedly. The dance floor was not crowded but was large, easily fitting hundreds of people. As the music changed, most of the dancers gathered in a close group. Sihanna, and many others, sang along as they danced. Many of the dancers were apparently celebrating, dancing and drinking wildly.

"I know how they feel," Sihanna messaged and screamed excitedly while she danced with exquisite turns and steps.

"It's been way too long," Allie messaged back and tried to keep up with Sihanna.

"Day's lovin' it," Sihanna messaged.

Allie looked around and saw Damien dancing in the midst of three Duarga women, all of them laughing and talking aloud.

After a few songs, Allie felt her throat getting dry. "I'm gonna sit. Thirsty," she messaged Sihanna and Damien.

"Yeah, me too," Sihanna replied.

Damien was already sitting, had finished the Rocket Fuel, and was now, drinking from a stein. He raised his glass as Allie and Sihanna sat. "Got thirsty."

People sitting at the table beside them passed as they returned from dancing. One of the ladies stopped between Allie and Sihanna, putting a hand on each of their shoulders. She was tall, and slender like Allie, and had the same short, blonde hair. She wore a light blue blouse, loose short blue pants, ending a little above the knees, and was barefoot. She leaned in, slurring and giggling every few words, "You look fantastic! I'm Ermenliebe. You must come join us; we are celebrating. After many years of struggle and strife, we have a new home."

Allie smiled and remembered the woman's *let it all go* joyous attitude when dancing. "I'm Allie!"

She and Damien got a message from Sihanna, "Yes, let's join them."

"I'm Sihanna!"

"Damien! Love to join you!"

"Wonderful! My name means wholehearted love, so I must hug you." She mashed Allie's and Sihanna's heads against hers and they moved to a new table, still beside the dance floor.

Allie messaged Sihanna, "You recognise her accent?"

"No. Athena's looking…Uruk Ashur…way down south, part of the Mirsinneen Wall. There's a war going on. They're evacuating the system."

"This is Liesel, Till, and Giselle. We are originally from Uruk Ashur," Ermenliebe said after they sat.

"Sihanna."

"Damien."

"Allie. From Lutetia Velum."

"Lutetia! We passed through the Lutetia system on the way here. All from there?"

"Yes, but Sihanna and I were born on Alesia. Damien was born here."

"So, you're coming home for a visit?"

"Sort of. My parents were working here when I was born. We moved to Lutetia when I was a year old."

Ermenliebe gulped from her glass, "Alesia, so you lost your home to war also. At least one of your childhood friends survived with you."

Allie chuckled. "We, ah…we didn't know each other on Alesia. We moved to Lutetia the same year. I was eleven, Sihanna was ten, but we didn't meet until eight years later. We all met the same night." Allie felt her lips drop into a deep frown as her stomach fell. "Yeah…five years ago, us three and…and another—" tears started flooding Allie's eyes, she blinked them back.

"We lost a dear friend recently, we all met the same night, about five years ago. He should be with us…but—" Damien's voice trailed off. He stared at his stein.

Ermenliebe raised her glass and said, "Then, you must drink, and dance with us. Tomorrow we leave for our new hab, our new home. All four of us come here alone. Each of us is all that is left of our families. Tonight, we drink, and we dance, for those who are cherished memories." She drained her glass.

Damien smiled as a server arm dropped a tray with seven glasses of Rocket Fuel

He picked one up and said, "To those who are memories," and then drained the glass.

Allie picked one of them up and gulped it down. Her mouth burned with fire, molten iron poured over her tongue, and a river of lava burned its way to her stomach. "Whoa.

That's hot." A quick, deep breath of air did nothing to soothe the burn.

Sihanna had put down her glass and was breathing heavily. "Forgot how strong that stuff is."

Their four new friends had the same reaction. When they returned their glasses to the tray, another tray, filled with glasses of Rocket Fuel, was set down.

Ermenliebe took a deep breath. "Delicious stuff. Burns hot like the rocket!"

Damien chuckled as he reached for another glass. "It is rocket fuel. It's three-quarters alcohol. Chemical rockets can burn it as fuel."

Ermenliebe drained another glass, stood and danced her way to the dance floor. "We dance! We dance until dawn! Whooo!"

***

Allie blinked and felt a pain in her head like it was being cut open. Thirst…oh, so thirsty. She lifted her head from the pillow and mumbled, "I'm in bed. What's wrong with my stomach? And my head, it feels like it's breaking apart."

"You drank copious amounts of alcoholic beverages last night," PAL-Allie informed her.

Allie rolled her head on her pillow and squeezed her eyes closed. "Ohhhhoohh…mmm. Don't use big words."

"Ya got shit-faced drunk last night."

"Ohhh…ah—" she said through deep breaths, "yeah, that part I know." After more deep breaths. "Feels like my stomach is trying to push food back up my throat. The pain in my head is unbearable. What's wrong? Why aren't you doing anything?"

"This is part of your officer training."

"What?"

"This is a training exercise, a one-day exposure to a toxic substance without med bot assistance. You haven't done this exercise yet. Last night gave us an excellent opportunity."

Allie felt her stomach tighten, convulse, once…twice…again, "You could've warned me. What's happening? What have you done?"

"Your med bots are in standby mode. Usually, when you drink, the med bots in your bloodstream clean out your system while you sleep and you feel no aftereffects. Last night, you experienced the natural effects of alcohol consumption, and today you will experience the natural effects of alcohol withdrawal, also known as a hangover…and I couldn't warn you. Part of the exercise is that it happens unexpectedly."

Allie's stomach convulsed again. "Augah…augah…augah—" Liquid and small chunks filled her mouth, spilt out, and covered the bed, then, again…and again…then, twice more. The first couple of times were mostly soft chunks, filling the space between her teeth and cheeks, under her tongue, on top of her tongue.

The chunks swished around in a sour, bitter liquid. Her throat burned. The taste was more sour and bitter each time. After a couple of heaves, there were fewer chunks and the liquid became thick and sticky, leaving long trails as it fell to the bed. The taste became more bitter than sour.

As she vomited, Allie desperately messaged PAL-Allie, "What's happening? What is this? Contact emergency services!"

"This is vomiting. A common symptom of alcohol withdrawal. The substance being expelled is coming from your stomach and is known as vomit. The liquid is the beer you drank, and the chunks are the roasted meatballs you ate last night. There is no real danger. The only permanent consequence will be the memory."

Sihanna woke up. "Allie! What's wrong?"

Oh no. I can't let Si know how bad this is, Allie thought, and said, "I'm okay. Just a training exercise."

"Damien, come quick! Something's wrong with Allie."

"I'm okay."

"Something came out of you!" Sihanna was in full panic mode, breathing heavily, holding Allie's arm.

Damien came running into the room. "What's wrong?"

"Hang on, I'm getting a message from PAL-Allie," Sihanna said.

"Me too," said Damien.

Damien and Sihanna looked at each other. Allie groaned.

"Athena, contact Mira," Sihanna's voice was filled with worry.

"Auagh…auagh—" Allie jumped off the bed and ran to the washroom, knelt before the toilet, and vomited.

The horrid, sour taste returned. This time the vomit was mostly liquid, and it burned her throat more. Less came up with each heave. The last two were almost empty, just a little slimy goo. She leaned against the wall.

"Allie?" Sihanna called out. "Are you okay?"

"I'm okay, Si. Just wanna rest here for a minute." Breathing heavily, she thought, *Yeah, the cool air feels good on my throat.*

"You should stay hydrated," PAL-Allie messaged.

"I just emptied my stomach. If there's nothing in there, then, I won't vomit again."

She felt her stomach convulse again; more vomit tried to come up, but there was none. After a couple of heaves, a little of the slimy goo came. "How…how am I still vomiting if there's nothing in my stomach?"

"This is just a common symptom of alcohol withdrawal. You will be okay. I have a file from Marshall Thabiti."

"No…no, you've made a mistake…something's gone wrong, I'm dying. I'm not gonna last the day…I gotta try and lie down…maybe I can sleep." She took a deep breath. "The file from Mira—"

"Not urgent."

Allie pulled herself up using the toilet for support. Her stomach was queasy. "Breathe…just breathe…okay. Little weak but not too bad. Gotta look strong, can't let Si know how bad this is."

Sihanna had removed the sheets. Allie flopped onto the bed, lying on her side facing the door. Mira and Aurelianus entered, grinning slightly.

"Gotta have a good ole hangover once in a while ta have some appreciation for the good things in life. I'll have one or two a year." Aurelianus chuckled.

Mira knelt by the bed. "How are you, Honey?"

"Horrible…my head feels like it's breaking in two…my stomach…ughhh—" Allie's stomach convulsed. She jumped out of bed and raced for the toilet, kneeling beside it. She tried to vomit while her stomach tightened, convulsed and heaved, but nothing came up. She leaned against the wall, breathing heavily, tried to vomit again, and again, each time leaving her stomach feeling like it was being forced out of her belly.

"Okay. I'm not gonna make it. I wanna make a video for Si."

"You are not going to die. Everything you're experiencing is common, temporary and will have no permanent effect on your health."

"No…something's gone wrong. Just help me make a video."

"Okay. What would you like to use as an avatar? A view of you from last night? Sihanna liked you in that skirt."

"No, I don't want to remind her of our last night together."

"Vacation last year? Got some great shots from the beach."

Allie felt her stomach convulse, something forced its way up her throat, burning, sour-tasting. Some kind of mash washed over her tongue. She spit it out and coughed a couple of times.

"Ahh...oh...no, not from vacation...cough, aaugh...aaugh...cough...cough...just use my uniform."

Allie saw an image of her dressed in a uniform like Mira's.

"Yeah...that's good...okay...ah...Si...Sihanna Calondda...It's been a great five years. I would've been lost without you. And...oh no! Now you're going to be alone...no. Si, find someone else, don't be alone, aaugh...aaugh, cough, cough, aaugh...don't include that coughing part."

"Okay, you should hydrate. It will help."

"Okay," two deep breaths, "Si! Can you bring me some water?"

Sihanna ran to the bathroom, spilling some of the full glass of water she had prepared.

Allie drank, the cool water washed over her tongue, doing away with the sour taste, and cooling her throat on the way down. It felt cool and calm in her stomach, so she gulped again, and again.

"Oh…oh, that feels better. Si—" She reached up with her arms for a hug. Sihanna took the glass, knelt, and hugged her. "I love you." Tears filled Allie's eyes, spilling down her cheeks.

"I love you, too. Allie—" Sihanna pulled back to look at Allie. "Athena tells me you're going to be fine. This is temporary, feels bad, but only lasts a day."

"I know." They hugged again and Allie took another gulp of water. "Feeling better. Let me go back to the bed."

She tried to stand but her stomach began to convulse. She turned back to the toilet just in time. Sour water filled her mouth and burst out. After a few heaves, she felt her stomach empty, but then her stomach tightened, convulsed, and tried to force something out, though nothing came. Her stomach tried twice more, and then she coughed.

"That was most of the water you just drank. You should hydrate again," PAL-Allie messaged.

"So, I can do THAT again! No, thank you, I'll just die dry."

"Allie? Are you okay? I…I couldn't watch," Sihanna called from the other room.

"I'm okay, Si, I'm gonna come lie down…soon."

Allie leaned against the wall, breathing deeply. "Feeling surprisingly better now. Maybe I will go lie down. I can finish the video on the bed."

"You'll feel better as the day goes on."

Her knees were wobbly, her legs shook, but Allie got to her feet, and the bed.

***

Allie blinked awake. Her throat was burning and dry, her head felt like it was splitting in two, and her stomach. "Ughhh…oh, yeah, hangover…guess I fell asleep."

"Allie?"

"Hmm?" Allie turned her head to find Sihanna sitting on the bed beside her.

"Feeling better?"

"Yeah," Allie yawned. "Where is everyone?"

"They went out for lunch."

Food. Allie's stomach was filled with panicked butterflies being chased by angry hornets, all crashing into the wall of her stomach. "Did you eat?"

"Yeah. I ordered something. I got you a sandwich, Athena's suggestion. Should help with the hangover."

"Ahh—" The thought of food stirred up the battle between the butterflies and hornets in Allie's stomach. "Maybe later."

Damien did not return until evening, chuckling when he entered. "How are you?"

"Better, but still have a headache, still a…funny stomach, but no more vomiting."

"Yeah…I learned about hangovers today. Did you know, before med bots, people got a hangover every time they got drunk?"

"Every time? No one would drink if they knew this was coming the next day…believe me…everyone would drink once, have a hangover, and then never drink again."

"Hmmm…a monthly night out was common."

"I can't believe you…that's like volunteering to have a hangover…never, not a second one."

"It's worth the hangover, was a common expression."

Allie stared at Damien. "No. Night. Out, is worth this."

She thought, *Should I tell him it's so bad I thought I was going to die? No.*

"*How are you feeling?*" PAL-Allie messaged silently.

"Better. Like I'm going to survive."

"*You were never in danger.*"

"Sure, felt like it."

"*Well, it's been a day, I'm bringing your med bots back online.*"

"It's over?" Allie felt a moment of elation, then caution.

"*Yes, you started drinking at this time yesterday.*"

Allie felt her head stop hurting, she felt more energetic, and her stomach…was empty. She whispered, "It's over."

"Huh?" Sihanna asked.

"The exercise is over, my med bots are back online, and…I'm starving." Allie felt a wave of euphoria. Her grin was unstoppable as she bounced off the bed. "Let's go eat."

Sihanna squealed, "Allie." And they hugged.

***

"So, if people got a hangover every time, and still drank." Allie plucked another meal pod from her plate, looked up at the nearly empty cafe, then at Damien. "There must have been a cure."

Damien gulped from his stein and swallowed. "Not really, water, orange juice, lime juice…all kinds of juices were tried, and believed to work, but—" Damien shook his head. "Nothing really worked."

"You don't feel like drinking anything. I have the feelings file, I'll send it to you," Allie said.

"Oh, that'll be great when I get back to class. And ahh, one cure sorta worked, having a drink or two."

"Ohh noo. No way anyone could drink." Allie shivered from the memory and put down her stein, no longer feeling thirsty.

"Didn't really cure the hangover, just reintroduced alcohol back into your system and suspended the withdrawal symptoms," Damien explained.

Thirst won, Allie picked up her stein and gulped some of the delicious stout.

***

The next morning, Allie opened her eyes, blinked, and realised she felt good. She laughed.

Sihanna woke, smiling. "What's so funny?"

"I just feel so great compared to yesterday."

"You look a lot better."

Allie smiled and thought, *Should I tell her how bad it was? No. She doesn't need to know.*

Allie felt Sihanna's arms encircle her and tighten into a hug.

"I sent her the video you started making," PAL-Allie messaged silently.

"WHY?"

"I talked to Athena and we both agreed that it was very sweet."

"You should've asked me! Must have been Athena's idea. I think she's a bad influence on you."

"Sihanna was very emotional when she learned you were thinking of her when you thought you were dying. She was also terrified when she thought someday she might have to face life without you...so, HUG HER BACK ALREADY!"

Allie hugged Sihanna.

"Glad that part of your training is over," Sihanna whispered.

"Yeah, me too, but now, I get a full Military assignment and I'll be a lieutenant by the end of the year. School will be done." Allie felt a surge of excitement. "Maybe the hangover was worth it." she giggled.

"Oh, you're already a lieutenant. All of us are. You should've gotten the assignment from Mira yesterday." Sihanna smiled.

Allie opened the file she received from Mira the day before. "Temporary field promotion to accommodate assignment to a classified mission."

Allie's heart rate quickened her lips curved into a smile, and then. "Classified mission...not exactly like it is in virch, eh?"

"Yeah." Sihanna chuckled. "So far all we've really done is wait for data searches...though I like the *fit in like a tourist* part."

Allie laughed with Sihanna. "Yeah, that's been fun."

"Hang on…Athena's back."

"Back?"

"Yeah, she went out last night, looking through data archives…she found something, wants us all to get together." Sihanna sat up and pulled the covers back.

"Okay, let's get dressed and contact everyone." Allie got out of bed.

"She already has. Damien is coming down the hall now." Sihanna jumped from the bed, went to the closet took out a robe, put it on, and handed another to Allie. "Okay, Day, come in."

Damien entered. "Morning. What's the news?"

"Don't know yet. Athena's waiting for Mira and Half Ton…they're here," Sihanna said.

As everyone gathered, Athena projected her avatar from Sihanna's wristband. She was a photo-realistic, light-skinned female with long black hair in a ponytail. She wore a dark red leather outfit with black trim, the top ending a little above the waist, the pants above the knee, and long boots coming up just below the knee. In her left hand, she held a blowtorch with a convenient carrying handle; in her right hand, she held a rod with a pistol grip handle.

"Ok, last night I found a puzzle room. Once I solved the puzzle, inside I found a lot of data about mass moving around. Gammarus hasn't been very honest about the data being collected."

Sihanna screamed a whisper. "Athena!"

Mira rubbed her forehead and sighed. "Huh, Honey—" She sighed again. "That sounds like an Imperial archive…send me the address, where'd you go?" After a brief pause, Mira continued, *"Sweetheart, that wasn't a puzzle room, or a game.* That, was a classified Imperial data archive. Has confidential information that can't be made public. Private information about people."

"Athena, you can't keep doing this." Sihanna folded her arms across her chest.

"The *puzzle* you solved was the archive security system," Mira said.

Athena tilted her head. *"Wha…no."* She folded her arms and stood on one leg. *"Hab needs a new security system."*

"That's ten years in a penal colony," Aurelianus said.

"I mean, really…you call that security?" Athena shook her head and wiggled her ponytail.

"It's Imperial security. Twenty years in a penal colony for breaking into an Imperial security archive," Mira said.

"Node Hack 3 had tougher puzzles," Athena said, shaking her head again.

"Athena, promise you won't do that again." Sihanna shook her head and sighed.

"Anyway, there's three thousand tonnes of anomalous mass—" Athena displayed a sketch of the hab, *"Right here."*

Everyone was silent. Mira finally spoke, "You know where we need to look?"

"Yeah, here, down in the reservoir level. Using the hab's water control and reservoir system, whatever is down there, can move around and get to any location in the hab."

Aurelianus looked at the section indicated, nodded, and said, "What are we waitin' fer?"

Chapter 7

"I'll have to requisition transport," Mira sighed. "Meanwhile, let's get some breakfast."

The entire day was spent in a futile attempt to find transportation.

"Militia only has two Saddle Wagons and they're both busy—" Mira complained during supper, "one skimmer, a Lusitano, that's available, but only seats four, and can only carry up to a ton of cargo."

"Why can't we use the cars? There's plenty of them," Sihanna asked.

"They don't have any skimmers. I've arranged for some skimmer bikes from a tour group. A few modifications are being made overnight. We should be ready to leave after breakfast tomorrow morning."

"No skimmer cars?" Damien eyes widened with surprise. "In the whole hab?"

Mira sighed and shook her head. "This hab is being used as an entry point for the swarm. Most of the people here are waiting for transport to another hab where they'll take up permanent residence. Only a few thousand physical residents live here permanently. No need for many cars. All bodies of water are small lakes or rivers; only skimmer cars are the Militia Lusitano and Saddle Wagons."

The next morning, Allie awoke to find a message from Mira. She nudged Sihanna. "We've got an hour to get ready, eat and meet Mira."

Sihanna woke and yawned. "Alright, let's go."

After breakfast, two cars took them to a Militia warehouse. Inside were six skimmer bikes and a Lusitano. The Lusitano was a skimmer car used by the Military and Militia, with a transparent bubble canopy atop a metal chassis with four wheels. Metal covered the back and top of the canopy and held the retracted back wings; a heavy machine gun was bolted on top. The retracted front wings poked out with a bump near the front wheels.

A battle bot sat under the canopy. The bikes had a high backrest that extended over the head. The extension held the retracted back wings; the front wings were in a pod over the front wheel. Two of the bikes were bigger and had double back wheels. All the bikes had a machine gun bolted atop the backrest extension.

"We'll use the bikes," Mira said. An image of the ring-shaped hab projected from Mira's wristband, with one section, highlighted. "There are three lower levels."

The image zoomed in and showed the levels. "The top two are hab infrastructure, storage, and…anything else needed…the lower level is the water reservoir, ten clicks wide, runs all the way around the hab in the middle, looks like a wide, shallow river. The water is used to support the biosphere above, but it's also used to control the hab spin. Along the sides are holding tanks."

"When mass needs to be moved to keep the hab spinning true, water gets pumped into the necessary tanks. But whoever, whatever, is hiding down there can't hide their heat. Link with the gun and sensors on your bikes. We'll take those ramps down." She pointed to a wide ramp sloping down. "The tops of the tanks are covered with stone brick; they can take our weight, no problem. We'll get up to skimmer speed and spread out over the water. Allie, eyes modification on."

Allie turned on the full spectrum receptors embedded in her eyes; she could see from infrared to ultraviolet.

"This is all I can get from the Militia. Gammarus isn't being very cooperative."

The canopy on the Lusitano opened and the battle bot stepped out. A torus laid flat, with six legs to move it, and a sphere mounted on top, nestled in the torus hole. Each side of the sphere had two gun barrels poking out from behind a shield.

"I got a message from Athena. She knows why the Militia is so busy," PAL-Allie silently messaged Allie.

"Why? Did she tell Si? How does she know?"

"Not important. The Militia is searching in the same area we're going."

"And how does Athena know this?" Allie sighed.

"Hmmm…she was busy last night."

"Open channels, everyone, full communication," Allie said. "Athena."

Athena's avatar emitted from Sihanna's wristband and stood among them. *"Okay, Militia and most of their equipment are already searching in the area we're going, and they're leaving a sensor trail."*

"And where did you GET this information?" Sihanna demanded.

"Ahh—" Athena puckered her lips, *"public archive…new duty assignments for Militia."*

"I've checked," Mira replied. "It's not there."

Athena puckered her lips on one side, raised her hands under her chin, made a fist with her left hand, and gently tapped her right palm. *"Ahh…mmm…and there are plenty of skimmer cars. Gammarus has them all in a warehouse on the other side of the hab."*

Mira held up her hand. "Athena." She sighed, scratching her forehead. "Can you get me access to those sensors?"

Athena's eyes widened, her lips curled into a big grin, and she clapped and nodded happily, her ponytail shaking vigorously. *"Oh yeah!"* her avatar retreated back into Sihanna's wristband.

"Oh no," Allie silently messaged PAL-Allie.

"Why?"

"Mira just gave Athena permission to hack a hab archive and Militia sensors."

"Yes, she did. You got a file from Marshall Thabiti."

"What is it?"

"You've been promoted to Commander, your security clearance has been upgraded to Secret, and you've been assigned to a new unit—the Imperial Security Battalion. Temporary field assignment to facilitate involvement in a classified mission."

Damien and Sihanna sent Allie the same message, "Did you get that?"

"Yeah, Imperial Security Battalion and ah…we're hacking local Militia," Allie said.

"Yeah." Damien grinned. "That's not ISB…that's Shadow Watch."

Allie's stomach churned with a mix of fear and worry. "This can't be good."

Thousands of stories, virch games, and videos were dedicated to the mysterious Shadow Watch. All of it rumour, speculation, legend, or myth…to be expected when the organisation doesn't exist. The Imperial Security Battalion is concerned with internal security and counterespionage and doesn't operate outside Imperial borders or violate Imperial laws.

Of course, no one believes this and, according to legend, Shadow Watch is the part of the ISB that executes these kinds of missions. The meme is so prevalent, that it's rumoured members of this secret, *non-existent* organisation have begun to refer to themselves as Shadow Watch. Confirming the rumour has not been possible.

Mira walked to the Lusitano and pulled some jackets from inside. "Put these on."

Allie slipped on the jacket and pulled the hood over her head. The jacket pulled together and joined in front, gloves extended over her hands, and a mask covered her mouth. Goggles rested atop the hood. She pulled them down over her eyes, and they melded with the mask, forming a complete seal over her face. Next Mira handed out wraparound skirts and slippers.

Putting on the skirts caused them to form into pants and join with the jacket. The slippers flowed over the feet and joined with the pants. The whole outfit puffed up a little. Mira handed Allie, Damien, and Sihanna a submachine gun, the same model they had found in the car. A long magazine poked out of the bottom of the grip. A backpack carried extra supplies.

"This armour is light, but it should stop rounds from the gun you're carrying and it gives you full environmental protection. Hopefully, we don't need it. It's cooler down there so no worries about being too hot wearing armour. Keep all communications open…mount up and roll out."

The battle bot got back in the Lusitano, and everyone else mounted a bike. Aurelianus used one of the bikes with two back wheels; the other was linked to Mira and carried extra power packs and ammunition.

Allie got on the seat, leaned against the backrest, and folded her arms. A canopy extended from the front wheel cover to the backrest, fully enclosing Allie.

"You okay?" PAL-Allic messaged.

"Yeah…no…why am I so nervous, we're just scouting." Allie's hands trembled, her breathing was sharp, quick, and short as she inhaled and exhaled.

"You're not just a little nervous. I'm detecting very high levels of adrenaline."

"Yeah. Scared shitless. I've been shot at, been in two real firefights. Didn't feel as scared as this."

"Both times were a surprise. Your training got you through it before the fear kicked in. Now, you know it could happen again, people could die and you're riding into it."

"Didn't really want to hear something so clinical. Deep breaths, yeah, deep breaths."

"You should wire the link for security."

"Where?" Allie asked.

"The seat beside your leg."

Allie held her arm beside her leg, the glove pulled back into the sleeve of the armour. A wire sprang out of her wristband and plugged into the edge of the seat.

"I've waited a long time for a real mission," Allie messaged PAL-Allie, she felt sweat roll down her forehead, sick in her stomach. "Can you do something about my stomach?"

"You'll be okay. Just a little nervousness before patrol. It's common."

"Yeah. Could use Mal's flask right now. Maybe a shot of rum would help."

"You need to be fully alert. Check weapons and sensors link."

Allie checked the link with the machine gun bolted to the top of her bike, and its sensors. "Checked."

"Ammunition and power."

Allie gripped the magazine. She held it tight to stop her hands from trembling, then snapped the magazine out of the grip, rested it on her lap, and pulled her backpack around her shoulder, taking out another magazine. She snapped it in, and checked the second spare. She took the power supply off the top and replaced it with another. She put the extra magazines and power supply back in the backpack and rested it between her legs.

"Checked," Allie said. Her stomach flipped a few times as her bike began moving.

The Lusitano took the lead and the bikes followed down the ramp. At the lowest level, they rolled along the top cover of the holding tanks to where it met the water. The edge was sloped and allowed easy access to the water surface for varying water levels.

"Full power along the edge to skimmer speed," Mira broadcast.

Allie was pushed back into the seat as the bike accelerated. The wings and jets extended, the jets quickly powered up, speeding the bike up to skimmer speed and it lifted off the surface.

"Let's get over the water, spread out, line abreast. Overhead lights will come on as we move," Mira broadcasts.

Allie noticed a heat signature in the distance, on top of the tanks. The butterflies in her stomach kicked up a storm and her fingers began to shiver. She messaged Mira, "Do you see that in the distance? Should we check it out?"

"Militia, searching along the tanks," Mira responded. "Athena's got me access to their sensor trail...and their communications."

Near the end of their run, Sihanna, nearest the opposite side, broadcast a message, "I got a signal. Weak, on top of the tank, near the water...lost it...we'll have to go back."

Allie's bike banked and turned, the wings tilted to maintain consistent lift.

The small fleet converged on Sihanna's bike. Everyone picked up the radio signal she had detected and skimmed over the surface of the tanks.

"Battle line, drop to wheels, follow me in," Mira broadcast.

The bikes and the Lusitano lined up behind Mira, dropped to the surface, and rolled to a stop a few hundred metres from the signal. They climbed out and the battle bot scurried to the front, walking insect-like on its six legs.

"Take your positions," Mira broadcast.

In her goggles display, Allie saw a white spot appear on the floor. They formed a line shoulder to shoulder then separated. Aurelianus was in the middle, to his left Damien and Mira, with Sihanna and Allie to his right.

"Damien, Sihanna, set to spray, Allie, laser grenade, Half Ton sandblaster, I've got the taser...everyone stay linked with your vehicle guns…two steps…hold—" Mira looked down the line. "We came here looking for something…and we found a signal drawing us in."

Aurelianus sniffed. "Sounds like a good plan for an ambush."

The battle bot moved forward, and Allie linked with its video feed. As it moved closer to the source, a small cube came into view. Dark red with black edges, about twenty centimetres on a side, with handles on two of the sides and a dark red gem set in the top.

"Yeah. That's it," Athena broadcast. *"Broadcasting a request for a link…but it doesn't respond, just keeps broadcasting a link request."*

A grey sample ring, half the cube height, rolled off the battle bot and bumped against the cube, deformed, flowed over, and covered it.

Mira read the results, *"Molecular seal. No anomalous chemical traces. Let's see if we can open the link. Athena?"*

Sihanna pulled back one of her gloves, Athena's avatar projected from her wristband, and stared in the direction of the cube. *"Oh, come on, work, will you…please just respond…OH, WILL YOU STOP BROADCASTING AND RECEIVE—"* After another minute, she started yelling in another language.

"What language is that?" Allie silently messaged PAL-Allie.

"Don't know, doesn't match anything in my database."

"Si?"
"Yeah?"

"What language was that?"

"None. She makes up her own swear words."

"Let's get closer. It's a short-range signal. Maybe we need to be right beside it," Athena said.

Mira looked to the cube, back to Athena, then nodded. "Okay, slow, spread out, ten steps forward and hold, weapons ready."

Allie held her gun to her shoulder, linked with her targeting system, zoomed in on the cube, and slowly walked forward ten steps. No changes were detected.

They slowly approached the cube until they were about twenty steps away.

Athena continued until she was beside the cube. She knelt beside it, slapped it, stared at it for a minute, pounded on the top, stared at it again, stood, kicked it, stared at it, looked up. "I'm out of ideas. It just keeps repeating a link request, but doesn't accept a *reply* to the request." She sat cross-legged beside the cube.

Allie zoomed in on the cube and came a few steps closer.

"Allie?" Mira asked.

"What if it needs to detect body heat and we're not close enough?"

"What if that's the trigger for a bomb?" Sihanna transmitted a cartoon image of an explosion.

"Too dangerous down here. Could damage the hab enough to cause catastrophic failure of the hab's structure. If destruction of the hab was their objective, they've had lots of time," Allie reasoned.

"Slow, any change, back off," Mira commanded.

Allie cautiously approached, knelt beside the cube, touched the handles, and tried to lift it, too heavy. Then she touched the red gem. It turned black.

Athena looked alert. *"It stopped broadcasting."*

Allie touched the black gem. It turned red again.

Athena stared at the cube. *"It's working! What did you do?"*

Allie shook her head and shrugged her shoulders. "Turn it off and on again?"

Athena's avatar changed to a cartoon version, adding a white lab coat and glasses. She pulled a spiral notebook and a pencil from the breast pocket of the lab coat, flipped through the pages, and stopped at a page marked *Unorthodox*. She already had a list:

Plead with it.

Yell at it.

Swear at it.

Slap it.

Punch it.

Kick it.

She wet the end of the pencil with her tongue and added to the list:

Turn it off. Turn it on.

She flipped the notebook closed, put it and the pencil back in the pocket, and reverted to her photo-realistic version. *"It's a data pack…with an encrypted message…I'm gonna need some time."*

"Sure, that thing is nothing more than a data pack?" Mira asked.

"Yeah, I've got complete access."

"Alright, let's put it in the Lusitano. Half Ton—"

Aurelianus put his weapon on his back, walked to the cube, gripped the handles, and tried to lift it.

"Heavier than it looks," he said.

He lowered into a squat, gripped the handles hard, and rose slowly. He stood, then slowly put it back down again. "Whooff, have ta bring the Lusitano closer." He wiped his hand across his forehead.

Mira lifted her goggles up, pulled down her hood and took a few steps toward Aurelianus.

"How heavy would you say that cube is?" she asked.

Aurelianus scratched his beard. "I can lift a half tonne. This weighs twice that or more."

Mira was now beside Aurelianus. She stared down at the cube and nearly whispered, "That can't be," then barked, "Jenny, get me Gammarus."

She pulled open her jacket at the top and started breathing rapidly with short, sharp breaths. "Use emergency channels," she said, as fear…no, terror, showed on her face.

Allie felt confused. "What's happening?" she messaged PAL-Allie silently.

"I don't know. She seems concerned about the weight of that cube…you got a file from Marshall Thabiti…your security clearance has been upgraded to Top Secret."

Mira shared her link with Gammarus. "I need all your Militia to converge on this location, and all Military assets mobilised for war."

Gammarus' avatar was a Human male dressed in a red and yellow tunic, sitting in an antique leather chair.

"Alright. But I should know why I have to call the Militia to active duty."

"They're already on active duty and deployed near us."

Gammarus raised an eyebrow "And, ahem, how would you know this, Marshall Thabiti?"

"And you need to execute Standing Order Twenty Two."

"Evacuate the hab? On what grounds? It isn't possible. This hab is a transfer point for ships coming from the wormhole and a major immigration point. We can't just shut it all down!"

"Gammarus! I'm exercising my authority under section seven three one of the Imperial Charter. This hab is now a war zone and under martial law! Failure to execute my orders can result in charges of treason and sedition!"

"First, I'll be filing my objections with the Imperial Charter Magistrate and the Imperial Trade Council. Then I'll request a lifting of martial law in the Supreme Court, and I'll be contacting Military Command—"

As he spoke, Mira played a video of a sidewalk at night, dimly illuminated by streetlights in the distance, and a closeup of a narrow alley. A black cat walked out of the shadows between the buildings, looked both ways with its black eyes, turned around, and walked back into the shadows. The video looped.

On seeing the video, Gammarus was visibly shaken. He looked afraid, confused, and uncertain for a few seconds before regaining his composure. He nodded. "Alright. Command of all Military and Militia assets transferred to you. Evacuation to begin immediately."

Sometimes legend and myth are more powerful than law. The black cat from the shadows motif was a well-known, pop culture icon for Shadow Watch and its more *notorious* activities. Mira had also openly transmitted her ISB identification.

"Allie! The water," PAL-Allie messaged.

Allie looked at the water. A long object, emitting a lot of heat, was under the surface moving toward them. Before Allie could speak, a large silver metal tube rolled out of the water.

A Lusitano rolled up and two Militia got out.

"What is that?" Mira raised her gun to her shoulder. "Maintain weapons and visual lock! Fall back!"

They walked backwards, maintaining eye contact. The long tube was made of joined sections. One end lifted and pointed at the Militia who had just arrived. A roar sounded. In a cloud of dust and debris, their Lusitano was blasted to pieces.

Damien and Sihanna fired near the raised end; sparks and electricity arced through the dust as the spray bullets exploded near the tube, releasing an EM surge and a cloud of glittering dust, temporarily blocking any sensors it used.

"Not gonna get a laser shot through that." Allie focused on a spot further down the tube where it rested on top of the tank and fired.

No damage, except the hole blown in the top of the tank.

The tube moved away from the spray shot and fired again. The battle bot was hit; more dust filled the air.

Allie couldn't see anyone or the tube. "SIHANNA, DAMIEN."

"Yeah."

"I'm good."

Aurelianus rushed past her. She heard the roar of his sandblaster. It stopped after a few seconds.

"It's gone back in the water," he said as he walked back through the settling dust.

He thumbed the controls on his weapon, a metre-long tube with a pistol grip and a foregrip. It had a short ammunition cylinder filled with sand-sized particles of iron hanging between the grips. Another cylinder, the power pack, was on top near the back. The particles of iron were magnetically accelerated to high speed and aimed at a target. It was a destructive, but short-range weapon.

"Mira's down!" Sihanna broadcast.

"Where are you?"

"Here."

Sihanna's infrared image cleared. Allie rushed through a cloud of dust. Mira was lying down, the armour and flesh on her lower left calf torn off. The exposed 'bone' looked like rough, dull grey metal with ridges running along its length. Several strands of rubbery plastic hung down from the top and bottom of the remaining flesh.

"Med bots got the pain and bleeding under control," Mira said, then reached down and joined the broken strands, the ends melding together when they touched.

Damien had retrieved the red and green med bag and ran to Mira's side, "You need anything from here?"

"Couple of med packs and a cooler."

Damien took two white med packs out of the bag and handed them to Mira. She pulled the remaining armour off below her knee and put the med packs over her wound. Damien handed her a plastic bag filled with liquid. She wrapped it around her leg just below her knee; it tightened and spread out to cover the lower half of her leg down to her ankles. She stood and tested her leg. She walked with a slight limp for the first couple of steps, then normally.

"Let's go check those Militia," she said. "Looked like they took a bad hit."

"Sure, you're okay?" Allie remembered Malik and how everything had looked fine when he got hit.

She smiled. "I'm fine. I'll just have a good appetite for a week while I regrow that tissue." She turned and started walking to where the Militia had parked.

"Wow," Sihanna messaged silently. "Did you see that? Cybernetic bones and muscles."

"Yeah," Allie replied. "That means she's as strong as Day?"

"Probably stronger. That missing tissue was fat and oxygen reserves. She can go days without eating and it would have no effect. She can hold her breath for hours…and her bones are a computer. Those fat reserves also act as a coolant if she wants to use either the computer or the muscles at high speed."

"What was that cooler pack?" Allie asked.

"It's just filled with water. Her med bots can work fast, heal the wound quick, and the water absorbs the excess heat. She'll have to empty it and refill whenever the water warms up, but lets her regrow her whole calf in a week."

The dust was slowly settling in the calm air. Allie saw both Militia down; their temperatures had dropped.

"They probably lost a lot of blood," PAL-Allie messaged.

Allie quickened her pace.

Sihanna ran past her, and knelt beside the nearest Militia, wearing the same armour as her. Part of their stomach on the right side was missing, a chunk was torn out of their right thigh, and their right leg below the knee was gone. The light armour had not been strong enough to stop whatever projectile had been fired but had lessened the damage.

Sihanna quickly put med packs on the wounds and moved on to the other soldier. The left side, from foot to neck, was shredded of flesh. Exposed muscle and bone were everywhere. Only the extra armour in the hood saved their head and their life. Sihanna started applying med packs.

"I'm out. Anybody?"

Allie checked her backpack, found three, and tossed them to her. After getting more from Damien and Mira, Sihanna finished covering their left side. She took a black strip from the bag, pulled up the damaged goggles, pulled down the hood, revealing a human male, and put the black strip near his forehead. She did the same for the other Militia, a Human female.

When Sihanna pulled down the woman's hood revealing her face, Allie felt a lump in her throat, and butterflies in her stomach. It was Corporal Jones, the woman they had met at the collapsed building.

"They're okay. There was no EM charge, just dead shot. I'm in contact with their PALs. They'll be up in a couple of minutes," Sihanna reported.

Mira looked at the residue. She took a bracelet-sized sample ring from her backpack and dropped it. It flattened into a square and slowly moved around, collecting samples of the dust and rock.

Another Lusitano rolled to a stop. A battle bot got out and scurried about the wreckage before standing near the water's edge.

Corporal Jones was sitting up now and trying to stand.

"You should sit. You're missing a lot of muscle and your right leg below the knee. You'll need to take it easy for a couple of weeks. Day, can you give me the splint?" Sihanna helped the woman sit, leaning to her left.

"How's...ahhh—" She took a couple of deep breaths. "Private Walker?"

"Little more torn up than you, but he's okay."

Private Walker stirred, rolled his head, opened his eyes and blinked.

"You're okay. Stay down. You lost some flesh on your left side got some broken ribs. You should lie on your back for now," Sihanna said as he tried to rise.

He nodded.

"Hey, we got a good one for a few days off, Joe," Corporal Jones said.

He chuckled. "Yeah."

Damien handed Sihanna a wide, shiny, silver metal strip. Sihanna pushed it against Corporal Jones' right knee. The strip melded to her leg and then formed into the shape of a lower leg. She stood and tested the splint.

She then nodded and smiled. "Yeah. That's good."

Private Walker chuckled. "Second time. Gotta stop losing that leg, Jonesy."

Sihanna smiled. "You've lost that leg before?"

Corporal Jones grinned. "Yeah." She sighed. "This'll be the second time regrowing that leg. Got torn off last year, little car racing accident, ya know the ones all our safety features are supposed to stop."

Private Walker roared with laughter. "Ya gotta leave safeties turned on if you want 'em to work."

Another Lusitano arrived and rolled to a stop near the injured Militia.

"Damien, can you help them get in?" Mira asked.

As Damien helped Corporal Jones and Private Walker into the Lusitano, Mira broadcast results from the sample ring.

"Rock. The bricks from the building, that collapsed. That's what was used for ammunition," she said.

"Are you sure?" Allie looked at the rock.

"Yeah, check the isotope comparison. Chunks of it hit us at high speed…that thing had us outgunned and retreating, then gave up the fight."

Aurelianus held up his weapon, "Only thing we had ta damage it."

"Yeah…guess that's it." Mira walked closer to the water.

Allie walked to her side. "What do we do now?"

Mira stared blankly out over the water and quietly said, "Battle bots are tracking that thing. It's waiting, about a klick out—" She looked at Allie. "We wait for reinforcements." She looked back to the water; fear returned to her face. "And if you have a god…now's the time to pray."

Chapter 8

Lights had been dimmed to simulate night. Tents had been set up, each defended by a brick wall on three sides, the side away from the water left open. The debris had been cleaned up, and the holes were covered with sheets of metal. A dozen battle bots stood guard.

Inside Mira's tent, bathed in candlelight, a nearly finished dinner of bread and spreads was laid out on a blanket.

"There was a transmission, between the Steel Snake and the cube."

"Steel Snake?" Mira smiled at Athena.

"Well. We need a name for it, and its shiny-like steel, long and round like a snake, points its head and attacks like a snake, so, Steel Snake. Anyway, I recorded the message; haven't been able to decipher it yet, though."

"Jenny, can help you with that. The *Steel Snake* hasn't done anything all day, it's just been sitting there. Some fluctuations in temperature, but otherwise no changes. No communication attempts…and nothing new from the cube."

"You said it fired rocks at us." Sihanna sipped her juice. "How do rocks do all that damage? I know it was light armour, but…wow."

"Chunks of rock moving at high speed," Mira said.

Allie chewed the last piece of bread, covered with a smooth, cheesy cream. "You seemed—" Allie shrugged her shoulders, "Afraid."

Mira nodded and cleared her throat. "Reinforcements are on the way."

"Yeah, I met Militia from Dal Riata Habitat, they were close by when you requested reinforcements," said Damien.

Mira tilted her head back. She sighed and stared ahead blankly, "I've ordered all Militia to leave as soon as the evacuation is complete. By then, reinforcements from ISB should be here."

"You know what we're facing?" Allie shivered.

Mira sipped her juice. "You know what Quantum Technology is?"

Allie nodded. "Yeah. Control of the subatomic, able to work directly with the nucleus of an atom."

Mira sipped again. "It's able to control the fundamental forces of nature," she sighed.

"Isn't it all theory, no real applications?" Allie spread cheese on another piece of bread.

"The Androids use it, the Obsidian Cyborgs, the ArConum…and us."

"So then, one of them is behind this," Damien shrugged.

Mira shook her head. "Not likely…there are others, but we're not sure how advanced they are…one of the substances that can be manufactured is monopolium."

"I've heard of that," said Sihanna.

"Yeah, me too. Usually, it's called polium in games," said Damien. "Incredible stuff, almost indestructible."

"Your games get some of it right. Takes a black hole or a Kugelblitz laser to damage it; bots made of it can go inside a star, can reflect all radiation, even gamma rays and X-rays, and has extremely high density…if that cube were a solid block of the densest natural metal, it would weigh less than a quarter ton; it weighs more than twice that."

"Inside the cube is a core of polium, and a power source. The core is impenetrable. The Steel Snake has access to technology we can't defend against…until reinforcements get here with the tech we need."

Allie's stomach churned and her lips trembled. "Who's coming as reinforcements?"

"A team from ISB. Should be here in a few days."

"A few days? How are they getting here so fast?"

"High acceleration ship. Meantime, by tomorrow some of the battle bots will be modified for underwater. We can stay close. If it moves, hopefully, we can track it."

The next morning, Allie's breakfast of nutrient bars was interrupted by a message from Sihanna, who was already up and out scanning the water.

"Athena and Jenny decrypted the message."

"Which one?"

"The transmission between the Steel Snake and the cube."

"I'm coming." She put the last of the bar in her mouth, pulled on her armour, opened the tent door, and met Sihanna, Damien, Mira, and Aurelianus by the wall facing the water.

They gathered around while Athena played a video. A solid white square on a black background, with a triangular notch on one side. A triangle slid in from the side to complete the square.

"A task was completed," Athena explained.

"Or a message delivered," Mira offered.

"That was a graphical representation…the intent of the message was that a task had been completed. Still working on the files downloaded from the cube."

"Ambushin' us," Aurelianus said.

"If ambush was the task." Mira rubbed her forehead and sighed. "Why such a brief attack that did little damage, and then retreat and hold position?"

"It's holding us here," Allie said, remembering some of her Tactics and Strategy exercises.

"Yes. Maybe it's also waiting for reinforcements." Mira looked toward their exit. "The underwater bots will be here soon."

An hour later, three battle bots arrived. One of them scampered quickly ahead, walking insect-like on its six legs. The ID it was broadcasting showed up in Allie's display:

Identity: Hari Fidela
Species: Cybernetic Intelligence
Persona: Human Male

Occupation: Captain, Homarus Habitat Defence Force, Imperial Defence Force at Har Megiddon Dyson Swarm

"Marshall Thabiti, it is the greatest honour of my career to get a chance to work with you. And my greatest horror it is under such dire circumstances. I am Captain Hari Fidela at your service." Captain Fidela lowered his front legs and spread his side shields at the bottom in his best interpretation of a bow.

"And a pleasure to meet you, Captain Fidela. I, too, wish our meeting were under better circumstances." Mira bowed.

"But endure we shall! And your young companions. To have lost and endured so much in such a short time and at such young ages. I am humbled by your service." Captain Fidela bowed again.

Allie felt compelled to bow in return. Sihanna and Damien followed suit.

Sihanna silently messaged Allie, "Is this a military ritual?"

"No. I guess he's…excessively polite?"

"These are two of my drones, BBHMDHH34 and BBHMDHH35, adapted for underwater work, armed with underwater sonic weapons. We shall have a closer look at this Steel Snake."

The two drones began walking into the water.

"I'll link you with their sensor feed," Captain Fidela offered.

Allie followed the drones' progress on video. In fifteen minutes, they stood beside the Steel Snake a few metres under the water's surface. The surface was smooth and impenetrable at the atomic level; confirming the surface was made of polium. Numerous communication attempts were made in multiple frequencies and methods.

"Nothing," Mira stated. "Anything on the message downloaded from the cube?"

Sihanna shook her head. "No. Athena's still working on it."

"Link with Gammarus. Some hab nodes are available now. That should speed things up."

Allie scanned the water. There was some heat, but no other radiation. She looked toward the cube…ambient temperature, still broadcasting a link request. She walked back to the wall and leaned against it.

Sihanna walked back and stood beside her. "Wanna grab a snack?"

"Yeah." Allie walked with Sihanna back to their tent.

As they stepped inside, she got a message from the battle bots. "Increase in temperature detected." They rushed out of the tent and back to the water.

Allie linked with the battle bots' video feed. Vision near the Steel Snake was distorted by the heat. The battle bots backed off as the water began to boil. With a roar and a cloud of steam and water, the Steel Snake began to speed along under the surface, leaving a wake of white, steaming water. It didn't travel far. It burst through the surface of the water, twisted in the air, and plunged end first into the top of the tank. It smashed through the stone-covered top, sending chunks of rock and a cloud of dust into the air. A white light shone through the dust and the end of the Steel Snake rose from the dust, engulfed in white fire. A windy roar filled the air. The white fire died and the Steel Snake fell back into the water with a splash.

"FALL BACK!" Mira yelled and broadcast, "Get on your bikes! Go! HALF TON! Where are you? We gotta go!"

As they sped away, she explained, "It's punched a hole in the outer hull. That roar, that's the atmosphere escaping."

Allie felt a shiver. "How much time do we have?"

"Gel packs will be in place to seal the hole before much atmosphere escapes. If the hole is small, we're fine, a big hole…the hab could break apart."

Allie shivered again as she looked back. "Ever been on a hab when it broke apart?"

"No—"

They retreated back to the Militia warehouse. A battle bot greeted them with a backpack hanging off of one of its gun barrels.

Mira took the bag and took five strips of cloth from it. She wrapped one around her left arm where it stuck to her armour, and handed the rest out. "Trackers. Make it easy for Search and Rescue to find us if the hab breaks apart and we get thrown into space. Your armour will give you five or ten hours."

"Okay…this is getting scary," Sihanna silently messaged Allie.

"Yeah." Allie nervously pulled on her armband.

Mira took a cable from the bag and wrapped one end around her waist, it stuck to her armour, she uncoiled some length. "Sihanna—"

Sihanna wrapped the cable around her waist and uncoiled some.

"Allie," Mira said.

Allie wrapped the cable around her waist and handed it to Damien, who did the same and then Aurelianus.

Allie's heart pounded...*bah-boom*...her breathing nervous...*bah-boom*...loud.

A terrifying metallic groan echoed through the warehouse.

Allie stopped breathing. There was no sound... a terrifying silence "Si?"

"Yeah," Sihanna whispered her response.

"Okay?"

"Yeah...we get ten hours, right?"

"Yeah, ten hours. Lots o' time."

"Are you remembering a virch?" PAL-Allie silently messaged.

"Yeah. Don't tell anyone it's only about a five percent chance of being thrown into space alive."

"I'm sure Marshall Thabiti knows."

"She probably does."

Allie increased the sensitivity of her audio sensors. No sound.

"The hole has been sealed," Mira broadcast.

Sihanna laughed and clapped.

No, don't message her, Allie thought, then messaged Mira silently, "Anything on the damage?"

"Small hole...less than a metre across." Mira's heavy, worried breathing was audible. "It's gotta be safe, Gammarus still has twenty thousand people to evacuate—" She switched to broadcast and continued, "Repairs have started. The hole is small and not spreading. We're safe."

Allie took a deep breath. She couldn't hold back a giggle.

Mira unwrapped the cable from her waist, rewound it, and handed it to Sihanna who did the same and handed it to Allie.

Mira said, "Keep your trackers on. Let's check that sensor trail. It can't hide down there."

Allie hugged Sihanna and Damien and linked with the sensor array. The Steel Snake had returned to its previous position.

After an hour, they returned to their campsite.

Inside their tent, Sihanna confessed, "I've never been that scared before."

Allie shook her head. "Yeah. All I kept remembering was a simulation I did, low chance of surviving a hab breakup...and when one hab falls apart, the pieces get tossed all about because of the spin." Allie displayed an illustration video as she spoke, "Those pieces hit other habs, they break apart, throw out more pieces...and eventually, every hab in the swarm can be destroyed."

"Sounds like a good plan for destroying a Dyson swarm."

"Yeah. Can stop it if there's enough balloon bots in orbit to collect the pieces before they collide with another hab."

The day passed with no further changes. The evening saw the lights dim and Allie leaning against the wall, sitting between Sihanna and Damien. She projected a video of a fire while they snacked on field rations.

"These things are—" Allie picked up a strip of meat. "This is...meat...of some kind." She dropped it back onto the tray, recalling the saltiness of an earlier one. "Are these cookies?" She picked up one of the white disks and tried to bite it. It was hard, so she bit harder, but it still didn't break.

Damien chuckled. "You have to soak those first—water, milk, melted butter, juice…lots of suggestions."

She tossed the disk back onto the tray. "The field rations on Lutetia were a lot better."

As Damien reached into his backpack, Captain Fidela scampered into the light of the video fire. He stopped, and his dim front lights illuminated Allie. "Commander Koibito." Damien pulled his hand out of his backpack as Captain Fidela turned to Sihanna, "Commander Calondda," and Damien "Commander Thorfinn."

"Captain Fidela. How are you?" Allie smiled.

He turned to the water, then back. "Alert. When facing so much uncertainty, maintaining our vigilance is the best defence we have. Reminds me of the time we were pursuing a clan of smugglers. Had to camp out like this, but in hiding, of course, in uninhabited habitats for months while waiting for them to make a drop-off. One night in Habitat three eight ss…oh, but I see I'm interrupting your supper."

"Enjoying our delicious field rations, are you? I've had many compliments on them. I've got a new flavour coming out next week. I'll see if I can get you a few in advance. Maybe for tomorrow's supper. Well, I won't bore you with my long story. Back to your meal. Must keep ourselves well-fortified. Good night."

"Good night."

When he had scampered out of sight, Damien pulled Malik's flask from his backpack.

"Damien! You can't have that here! You want to face a court-martial!" Allie exclaimed.

Damien shrugged his shoulders. "It's Mom's birthday." He took a sip from the flask and handed it to Allie.

Allie took the flask. "This is really not a good idea...but—" she took a sip, barely enough to swallow. The harsh rum burned her tongue. She handed the flask to Sihanna, nervously looking about.

Sihanna took a sip and handed the flask back to Damien.

"We'll save the rest for a better time." He shook the flask and said, "Still half full." Then, put it in his backpack.

Allie sighed. "Mal wouldn't have liked it here right now. Everything shut down, everyone evacuated, and we stuck down here."

Damien chuckled. *No rum.*

Mal, no rum, can't imagine that, Allie thought and chuckled. "He would have found a way to get rum...and tobacco."

Sihanna and Damien laughed with her.

"He would have loved that salty meat, though," said Damien.

"Yeah, he really liked salty stuff, didn't he?" Sihanna nodded.

"Yeah." Damien smiled. "Misty Isles does all Gaian farming and fishing. Everything is natural. A lot of the food is just salted and dried for preservation."

"No refrigeration?" Sihanna asked.

"Yeah. Just not for everything. Some of it is exported. Big market for Gaian food. Gaian markets in general. Wood, for example, is so much easier and faster to grow in an organic fabrication pod. But there's a huge market for naturally grown wood from trees. Used for houses, boats, furniture, almost no market for fabbed wood. And tobacco."

"Hundreds of varieties with any drug you want, but all grown naturally…and we smoke it in a pipe and light it with a match, the most ancient way we can smoke." Damien sighed. "A bit strange, really…but with so much tech in our lives, guess we need to remind ourselves we're natural beings, Gaian creatures…still just part of the cycle."

Allie nodded, savouring her memories of flavours. "Hmmm, it's delicious to have real food…we get our real bacon from Misty Isles."

"Hmmm…yeah." Sihanna smiled. "And real ice cream and real chocolate—" She closed her eyes and licked her lips. "And real buttercream for real waffles with real blackberries—"

Allie's mouth watered. Her stomach growled as delicious memories flooded her tongue. "Sihanna!"

"What?"

"Stop."

Sihanna chuckled, and asked deviously, "*Whyyy?*"

Allie closed her eyes and sighed. "Hey, tomorrow we'll probably get time to go back to the warehouse. There's a park behind it, lots of meal bushes."

Sihanna smiled. "Yeah, count me in."

Damien nodded. "Sounds delicious."

***

The next morning Allie was awakened by Sihanna excitedly speaking into her ear.

"Allie…Allie…Athena's deciphered the downloaded message!"

"Hmmm—" She took a deep breath. "Okay, I'm up."

She sat up, Athena was standing beside the door of the tent, blowtorch and rod in hand, switching the blowtorch on and off as she stared absently ahead.

Allie pulled her hood up, pulled the goggles down, picked up her weapon, and followed Sihanna and Athena outside.

Everyone gathered around Athena. She spoke aloud and broadcast with some graphics, *"So it looks like it used DNA as a random number generator to create an encryption key. Mostly what we have is a lot of observations and data. Observations and records of habs, their physical description, orbits, a lot of attention to the balloon bots and the stellar husbandry swarm. And ahhh—"* she paused and looked at Mira, *"The Steel Snake is a Mirsinneen avatar."*

"How can you be certain?"

"I've compared the—"

"Wait." Mira pulled back one of her gloves. "Jenny."

Jenny expanded from Mira's wristband, a light-skinned, blonde human female, wearing a light pink t-shirt, trousers, and sandals. Mira looked at her.

"She's right. We compared the data structuring and the code used to run it. The picture and video formats match, numbering sequences—" Jenny shrugged her shoulders. *"I've sent everything to Command for further analysis."*

"That means—" Mira paused.
"Mirsinneen has Quantum Technology," Jenny said.
"This message hasn't been delivered yet," said Athena.

"It hasn't," agreed Jenny.

"It's been encoded in someone's DNA. The person is delivering the message personally." Athena laughed at her attempt at humour and fired a long blast on her blowtorch.

"You're certain?" Mira looked at Athena, then Jenny. Both answered yes. "Because if Mirsinneen is waiting for this message before launching an attack…and it hasn't been transmitted yet…wait. How did it get into someone's DNA? Whose?"

"I don't know," Athena answered.

"And if we checked everyone here?"

Athena looked around, nodding. *"Yeah, could be someone here. You wouldn't know. And the message could've been inserted—"* she tapped her chin with her finger. *"Maybe when you were sleeping…by a Q-tech bot swarm, we wouldn't have detected it…and it wouldn't affect you. At least not right away."*

"Alright. Sihanna, DNA scanner." Mira pulled down her hood.

Sihanna took a short silver and black rod from her backpack, held one end against Mira's cheek for a second, clicked a button on the other end, and pulled it away.

"Should only take a couple of minutes," Sihanna said as she put the rod in her bag and took out another.

She took her hood down, pulled it back from her cheek, and took a sample. She held the second rod for a minute, then took the first out and put the second in her backpack.

"Transmit the results to Jenny and Athena when you get them," Mira said.

Sihanna nodded. After a few minutes, all had their DNA sampled.

With a deafening roar, the Steel Snake bounded into the air. Spinning and turning, it fired hundreds of grenade-power laser blasts all around.

Several hit near Allie. Holes were blasted in the top of the tank; pieces of the rock brick covering it were thrown out by the blasts. Several hit Allie. Fortunately, they were small and not moving fast, her armour held.

There was dust everywhere. A cloud of exploding spray bullets erupted around it, coming from the battle bots below. The spray effectively blocked the Steel Snake's sensors and it stopped firing. White flames fired from one end and it shot away.

"Check in," Mira broadcast.

"Commander Koibito. Check in."

"Commander Calondda. Check in."

"Commander Thorfinn. Check in."

After a pause, Mira broadcast, "General Riothamus, check in…spread out, let's look for him."

Allie walked between the tent enclosures toward the water. There were holes everywhere beyond, and pieces of rock strewn about. The dust had thinned a little, but visibility was poor. She lifted her weapon in front as she moved into the open. Her display flickered. Then again.

"I'm going to—" PAL-Allie messaged.

"To?" Her display continued to flicker.

"Ing to…art."

"I didn't get your message," Allie messaged PAL-Allie.

"Restart. I'm going to restart. I'm not sure…something's happening, a restart should fix it."

"Si…Si? Si, are you there? I might be offline for a few minutes. PAL-Allie has to restart."

Sihanna rounded the tent enclosure and stepped into the open.

"Allie? Are you online yet?" Sihanna switched to infrared and scanned through the dust. "Day. You see Allie?"

"No, her signal's not back yet."

"Converge on her location. Marked," Mira broadcast.

Sihanna saw the location marker flash in her display and walked toward it.

"Weapon up, ready to fire," Athena silently messaged, and pulled back a glove to show herself walking beside Sihanna.

Sihanna noted Damien and Mira's position as she closed in on Allie's location. She was near the space between two tent enclosures. Somebody was down, their upper half hidden between the walls.

ALLIE! she thought the scream, too scared to speak.

She sprinted to Allie and knelt beside her, lifted her head, pulled up her goggles, and tugged at her uncooperative hood, only managing to pull it back from her face. Her PAL still emitted no signal.

Sihanna took a black strip out of her backpack and draped it over Allie's forehead.

"Pull my other glove back, Athena." Sihanna's fingers trembled as she adjusted the strip.

"Mira just got a message," Athena messaged silently.

"How do you know?"

"I'm tied into hab communications. The people on this hab were having some very strange conversations."

"Why are you reading people's private messages? Never mind, help me with this. Why does this look so…random?"

"It's not a brainwave pattern. Looks like random magnetic fluctuations after an EM attack."

Sihanna pulled her goggles up and her hood down. Her lips trembled. "Allie, wake up." A lump grew in her throat. "Allie, it's time to wake up." Her hands were shaking, her voice quivering. "Allie, please wake up…Allie, wake up."

She cradled Allie's head in her hand and lifted her to hug. She pulled the hood down more. A dried piece of Allie's scalp came off in her hand, the dull white bone of her skull visible. Sihanna's whole body shook, her voice desperate, pleading, "Allie, wake up! Allie…ALLIE…WAKE up." Her tears started flowing as her voice dropped to a low squeal, "Allie, please wake up."

Athena knelt beside Sihanna, and put an arm around her shoulders. *"I have a video, recovered from a destroyed battle bot. It shows Allie—"*

"Show me." Sihanna had begun sobbing.

"Are you sure? It's not good."

She wiped away a few tears. "Play it."

The video showed Allie walking out from between the tent enclosures, and Aurelianus waiting outside the wall. He pointed a large disk at Allie and pulled the trigger. A few sparks flashed off Allie's armour and she fell. Aurelianus turned toward the camera and fired again. The scene cuts to a black screen.

"Looked like an EM or microwave blaster," Athena said.

Sihanna felt cold and numb. "Was that…did he—" Shaking more now, she put Allie down. "Where is he? Can you track him?"

"I can pick up his tracking signal. He's running that way."

An arrow showed the direction in Sihanna's display. Her stomach boiled, her hands shook, her lips quivered. There was too much anger to cry. She picked up Allie's gun. "Bring the bike."

Sihanna started walking in the direction of the arrow. Her anger surged and she started to jog. The pressure built in her stomach like something was boiling inside.

"Die." She started running. "DIE." She was running faster. "YOU WILL DIE!"

The bike came up beside her.

She slowed, jumped in the seat, and the canopy closed. She linked with the machine gun bolted on top. Its targeting view came on in her display. She selected armour-piercing rounds and locked on to an infrared signal in the distance.

Athena appeared sitting in front of Sihanna. *"That's not the real Half Ton. The message Mira got was about his DNA scan. This is an organic bot made using Half Ton's DNA."*

She was close enough now to see him, running.

"Can't get too close. He's armed," Athena warned. *"Still got that sandblaster, at close range that'll tear us to shreds. And if he hits our power supply with his machine gun, we'll blow up."*

Athena slowed the bike, turned away, and circled back. Sihanna marked his legs as a target and fired a ten-round burst. At least one bullet found its mark and he fell. Athena circled around for another shot as he got up.

Sihanna fired another burst and knocked him down again. This time the bullet took off his left leg below the knee. He stood again, defiant, gun in hand, and fired. Athena turned the bike sharply several times, avoiding most of the bullets. A few bounced off of Sihanna's armour.

"Your puny bullets can't hurt me. Give me another shot, Athena. We'll just blast him apart piece by piece."

After a couple more passes, the Aurelianus bot had lost both legs below the knee, was lying on his back, and had stopped firing and moving.

"Sihanna, he's down," Mira messaged.

She pulled her bike alongside Sihanna.

"Not dead yet."

"Yes, *it* is. It's safe to stop. Let's get a closer look."

Athena guided the bike to stop a few steps from the Aurelianus bot. Sihanna got off the bike and stood beside the shattered remains. The bullets from the machine gun had torn holes in the armour. The flesh underneath was already dried and breaking apart. Chunks of red and brown had fallen out where the legs had been shot off.

"Same thing every time we get close to getting one." Mira was standing beside Sihanna. "They decompose before we can get any info. The real Half Ton is on his way here. I didn't know this was a bot until a few minutes ago."

"I know." Sihanna couldn't stop staring at the remains. Her stomach boiled, filled with pressure. She stepped backwards to her bike, raised Allie's gun to her shoulder, held it tight, selected the bot as a target, and fired. She fired a dozen bursts, emptying the one-hundred-round magazine.

When it was empty, she lowered the gun. Mira was standing beside her, putting an arm around her shoulders. Sihanna turned to her and Mira embraced her. Sihanna dropped Allie's gun, and embraced Mira, sobbing at first, then crying loudly.

"I know, Honey…I know," Mira quietly whispered.

"Allie!" Suddenly Sihanna remembered she had left Allie alone.

"Damien's with her."

"Let's go back." Sihanna couldn't stop her sobbing. She picked up Allie's gun and got on her bike.

"Athena, help me," she messaged silently as she rode.

"I am…and a little more info I haven't shared with everyone yet. The Steel Snake is just programmed. Good programming, but that's it. No independent thoughts or actions. A dead computer, with a backdoor. And I have the key."

"What?"

"I can hack the Steel Snake. That's what killed Allie. The Aurelianus bot was just a drone being controlled by the Steel Snake."

"Are you sure, Athena? This is a Q-tech computer, a lot more advanced than anything you've hacked before."

"Still operates on the same information theory principles, just faster."

Sihanna looked at Mira's bike ahead. "Don't tell anyone, they'll just try to stop us. Wait until everyone is asleep…and we attack."

Athena played a short video. She was standing, holding her blowtorch and rod. She raised her arms triumphantly, a huge grin on her face. Flames shot from the blowtorch, lightning from the rod.

Chapter 9

Sihanna woke with a quick, sharp breath, lying on her back.

Oh yeah. Athena put me to sleep. She turned her head. *Allie.* Tears filled her eyes. She sat up and wiped her tears. *No time to cry now.* She leaned down, and kissed Allie on the forehead, all the while feeling her stomach boiling. "It will pay. It will die," she whispered, she picked up Allie's gun, got up, and went outside.

Athena followed her out. *"Mira and Damien are asleep. There are a few battle bots on guard. They shouldn't bother us."*

"Okay. What next?"

"Let's get closer to the water. I'll have a stronger signal."

Sihanna walked close to the water's edge. She heard walking behind her.

"Good evening, Commander Calondda."

"Tell him you're out for a walk, couldn't sleep," Athena messaged silently.

"Captain Fidela. I couldn't sleep, thought a walk might help."

"Understandable. Not to worry. My bots will keep a sharp eye on the Steel Snake. Any change and we'll be ready."

Sihanna nodded and Captain Fidela scampered away.

"I'm ready," Athena messaged.

"Show me."

"Hmmmm...okay."

Sihanna's entire field of vision was filled by a grey wall covered in ones, zeroes, and decimals. There was a blank space in front of her.

"I just have to write the key here and we're in," Athena said, pointing to the blank space.

"You have the key?"

"Yeah. It's Damien's DNA. I just have to write the zeroes, ones and decimals in the blank spaces and we're in."

"How did it get Day's DNA?"

"Don't know. But we might find out when we get in."

Athena turned to the wall and aimed the rod.

"Stop, Athena. Wait," Mira said aloud.

Athena cut the simulation video. Sihanna's vision returned to normal.

Mira was beside her. "Not now, Sihanna. We may only get one chance to use this. We have to wait."

Sihanna growled. "It KILLED Allie!"

"I know how you feel—"

"YOU DON'T!"

Sihanna held Allie's gun in one hand; tears started rolling down her cheeks.

Mira stepped closer, clasped both her hands around Sihanna's free hand, and whispered, "Sihanna, Honey, I've lost a loving husband and two wonderful children to war. I know how you feel."

Sihanna started sobbing.

"I've also lost a lot of friends doing what you're doing now, running off, angry, looking for revenge."

Sihanna dropped Allie's gun, put her arms around Mira, her head on one of her shoulders, and cried.

***

In the morning, Sihanna woke up in her tent. Allie was beside her. Sadness filled her, sadness so dark she wanted to cover her head and go back to sleep.

"Athena."

"I'm here."

"I need to sleep some more."

"You should get up. Eat something."

Sihanna's stomach rebelled at the thought of food. "Not hungry."

"Something to drink?"

"Not thirsty."

"You need to drink. You're dehydrated."

Sihanna's tears pushed against her eyes, but they got stuck. They were there, struggling to get out...one little one finally managed to fill the corner of her eye. She felt dryness in her throat.

"I don't have any tears left. I guess I should get something to drink.*"*

She got up and went outside to one of the food and drink lockers. She found a bottle of goji juice and quickly gulped half of it down. She felt hungry and grabbed a field ration. She tore the small tab off the side to start the warming cycle. She sat by the locker and leaned against it as she waited for her meal to warm.

In a few minutes, the top popped and she peeled back the cover. Bacon, eggs, and toast.

Don't remember checking to see what it was.

She put a strip of the bacon in her mouth, then chewed and swallowed.

Why are these so salty?

She used the fork to sample the eggs. Their saltiness dominated the flavour. She tossed the fork back on the tray, picked up a piece of toast and tried it.

Yep. Even the toast. Covered in salty butter.

She tossed the half-finished slice of toast back on the tray and took another gulp of juice.

"Hey, Si." Damien took a bottle of juice from the locker and sat beside Sihanna.

"Morning, Sihanna." Mira was holding a body bag.

Sihanna felt her tears coming again. Her breathing quickened, her stomach burned, and her heart pounded. "I guess we have to—" she sobbed, "Can we take her back to Udara? Bury—" she sobbed again, "with…with Mal?"

Mira knelt beside her. "Yes, Honey, anything you want."

"But let me and Mira put her in the bag," Damien said.

"No. No, I want to—"

"Si, Please don't," Damien pleaded.

"Honey." Mira took both of Sihanna's hands in hers. "She was hit with a high-power microwave blast. There's a lot of tissue damage on her back. You have a lot of great memories together. Please, trust me—" Mira paused and wiped a tear, "you don't need to remember her burned body when you think of her." She gave Sihanna a hug. "Let Damien and me transfer her, but first, come inside with us. We'll get a lock of hair."

Inside the tent, Damien handed Sihanna the scissors. She knelt beside Allie, still in her armour, and reached toward her hair. Sihanna's hands started shaking.

"Athena."

"Got you."

Her hands steadied. She lifted a lock of hair and cut it. Tears burst forth and she cried loudly. Damien knelt beside her. She leaned into him as he embraced her. She held out the scissors. Mira took them and looked at Damien. He nodded toward Allie. Mira cut off a lock of hair and handed the scissors back to Damien. Sihanna slid back to the wall of the tent and sat. Damien cut off a lock of hair and took his locket out of his pocket. Sihanna pulled hers up by the chain around her neck and opened it. Her hands started shaking again.

"I'm on it," Athena messaged silently.

Sihanna's hands stopped shaking. She opened the locket and put the hair inside, laying it across Malik's hair. She closed it, dropped it, buried her face in her hands, crying, tears flowing. "Allie…noooo …Allie."

Damien sat beside her and hugged her.

After a couple of minutes, she wiped away her tears. "I'm okay." She crawled to Allie, kissed her forehead, lay across her chest, and hugged her.

She stood, wiped her tears again, and looked at Damien. Then she nodded and said, "Okay," before walking outside.

"It's a Mirsinneen avatar?" she asked Athena silently.

"The Steel Snake? Yes."

"So Mirsinneen is behind all this?"

"Yeah."

I didn't check Mal for organ failure, and if I'd stayed by Allie's side— Sihanna took another bottle of juice from the locker and sat beside it. "Athena, show me more about Mirsinneen."

Over the next few hours, Sihanna learned Mirsinneen was composed of balloon bot units, surrounding fifty thousand stars. Every star had a wormhole and everything was connected into a single hive mind. The Mirsinneen War broke out when expansion brought the entity into several inhabited star systems. First to respond were the Androids, an organisation of swarm bots that used human-form bodies. They fought most of the war, destroying Mirsinneen swarms in dozens of star systems. More systems joined the war, but the Mirsinneen swarms were relentless. The Androids artificially induced several stars to go supernova to destroy Mirsinneen strongholds.

Peace was had when Mirsinneen agreed to stop expanding in most directions, while the forces allied against it agreed to stop *killing the stars*.

"How do we kill it?"

"Wow. That's a lot to kill, but—" Athena showed herself sitting beside Sihanna. *"If we had construction templates and a construction swarm, all we would need then is a ship to take us to an uninhabited star system and we could build whatever we need."*

"Can you get that?"

"Got access to everything in the hab right now...hang on." Athena stared blankly, then nodded. *"Got it. Got a construction swarm from hab stockpiles, and construction templates...there's a full Imperial archive. Just have to decide what we need...there's a lot here...we'll just take everything...it's going to take too long to copy. I'll get one of the battle bots to take the memory packs used for backup."*

"Athena, what are you doing?" Butterflies danced in Sihanna's stomach, her lip trembled. "Wait. You're raiding an Imperial archive…Do you have control of all the hab systems?"

"Yes. Gammarus is not very good at security…relax, I'll just…hmmm…hang on—" Athena began to hum as she stared blankly ahead. *"Skolto might be available…and I've got hab nodes…okay, he doesn't want to cooperate, well…I'll just cut the power—"*

"Athena, what are you doing?"

"We're going to need a ship and Skolto is here. Just have to…okay, got control of a bot…power is cut…Skolto is offline."

"Sleeping."

"It's more like being dead."

"Dead! Athena—" Shock and horror filled Sihanna's body, she started shaking.

"Relax. Not dead forever, just until I power everything back up. I'm just going to make sure Skolto doesn't cause any trouble. I just need to insert a few lines of code here and there…and we'll have the ship we need."

"But you're—"

"Just relax. Skolto will be fine…and will be doing the same thing as the last thousand years…I'll need a few minutes."

Athena cut her display and her image disappeared.

Sihanna spent most of the day in her tent, sleeping, crying, eating little. After a night of restless sleep, she met Mira and Damien for breakfast.

Sitting on chairs outside her tent, Mira handed Sihanna a bowl. "Oatmeal with berries."

Sihanna tried a spoonful. The warm oatmeal flowed over her tongue. When she chewed, the berries spilt their delightful flavours.

Mira cleared her throat. "Jenny sent the results of the DNA scans to Command. There they spotted the difference between the bot's DNA and the real Half Ton. Was a good job, and good timing. While Half Ton was visiting his home system, Shylow, the bot showed up at Udara Seven."

"Programming was good. There was no one who knew him well enough to spot any differences. I haven't seen him in over thirty years." She sighed. "Fooled me easy enough."

She dropped her spoon in her half-finished bowl of oatmeal and set the bowl beside her chair. "Mirsinneen was gathering information about the Dyson swarm. The treaty that ended the Mirsinneen War stated that we were not going to kill the stars."

"Mirsinneen will believe we're killing the star because we're lifting mass off it. That's gonna lead to another war. And if Mirsinneen uses Q-tech this time—" she sighed and shook her head. "It will be bad…the destruction, unimaginable."

"Yeah. The stars are like its religion," Sihanna said, not really recalling a lot of the facts of the videos from the day before.

"More like a philosophy than a religion...based on observation. Life Bringers, it calls the stars. The stars energise the universe; without the stars, there is no life. We are killing a star, so we must be stopped."-

"But we're not killing the star," said Damien. "We're stopping it from going supernova and killing billions."

"I know. The observations show us taking mass from the star. Yes, that stops it from going supernova and extends its life, but also lowers its energy output. When we agreed to stop killing stars at the end of the Mirsinneen War, we believed stellar husbandry, like we're doing here was exempt."

"When it became clear that Mirsinneen believed otherwise, and refused to negotiate the point, we hoped dense swarms would mask our operations. Guess Mirsinneen found a way to get a closer look. We're forcing this star to lose mass and lowering its energy production, so we're killing it. That's what Mirsinneen sees, not the future supernova."

"Couldn't we teach it about supernovae?" Damien asked.

"It trusts only the data it collects from its own observations, and apparently has never seen a natural supernova."

"So, there's a war coming. And Mirsinneen wants to destroy Har Megiddon," Damien said.

Mira nodded slowly. "Yeah, looks like it. And it will probably conclude every Dyson swarm in the Empire is killing a star, and fight with Q-tech…just fighting the battle for the swarm will destroy it. Launch the attack and its mission accomplished."

After breakfast, Sihanna spent some time in her tent.

Athena emitted from her wristband and sat beside her. *"Getting Skolto loaded with everything we'll need. Lots of minerals and metals we can use."*

"Are you raiding an Imperial stockpile now?"

"I'm not raiding, just moving it to a secure location. Skolto is Militia and needs to ensure resources are available for the current crisis."

"How is Skolto? Back online?"

"Oh yeah." Athena held her hand palm up, and a kitten, white with black spots walked onto it. A patch of silver fur formed a *S* on his forehead. She said in a childlike voice, *"E's my widdle kitty."*

"Athena! What did you do?"

"Relax, it's just a new avatar."

The kitten turned and walked away, fading out of view after a few steps.

"When we're ready to leave, you just need to get to Skolto. I'm going to transfer over and run from the computer substrate there. I've got the hab communication network to maintain connection with you. And…you know…if something happens to you…I'll be safe."

"Okay." Sihanna lay back on her sleeping bag. "I wanna have a nap now. Put me to sleep."

"Okay."

A few hours later, Athena woke Sihanna. *"Wake up! Wake up!"*

"What?"

Athena was standing near the tent door. Her hair was a mess, there were black marks on her face and hands, and her clothing was torn in a few places. She grinned broadly and giggled as she spoke. *"I've been inside."* She tried shooting her blowtorch, but it just belched a small ball of flame and some black smoke before going silent.

"Inside where?"

"The Steel Snake. I used the backdoor key."

"Athena!"

"It's okay, really." Athena continued to giggle intermittently.

"You look terrible."

Athena giggled and looked down at her clothes. She dropped her blowtorch and rod, shook her hair, and tied it into a neat ponytail. She rubbed her hands together and rubbed her face clean. She pushed the torn clothing together and it rejoined. She picked up her blowtorch and rod, test-fired the blowtorch, and got a satisfactory flame shooting out. She lost the wide grin and giggle. *"Wow. It's chaos in there. But I got an egg from it."*

"An egg?"

Athena held her hand in a cup shape. A small silver ball appeared. *"Looks like this. It's a ball of polium. Bots are taking it to Skolto. Gonna have to explore it to see what it does exactly."*

"Athena! You took unknown tech to Skolto?"

"Relax. It's fine. I can use it as computronium, really fast computing."

"You said you didn't know what it was."

"I know basically what it is, just not its full capabilities."

"Athena, I think you've made a big mistake."

A loud roar sounded from outside. Sihanna pulled up her hood, put her goggles over her eyes, picked up her gun, and rushed outside.

The Steel Snake was in the air, blue and white flames streaming from one end while it blew large holes in the top of the tanks with powerful laser blasts.

"Get to your bikes!" Mira yelled.

"Wait! I can get in! I can stop it!" Athena broadcast.

The Steel Snake had roared further away, making a line of holes.

"Next it's going to blow holes in the outer hull and destroy the hab. I can stop it!" Athena broadcast.

Mira looked distracted for a minute, then alert and speaking rapidly, "Help is almost here. Let's fall back. There's a transfer pod at the Militia base. It'll take us to Skolto. We'll be safe. Let's go!" Mira rushed to her bike.

Sihanna ran to her bike, got on, and closed the canopy. "Athena."

"I'm here," Athena projected herself sitting in front of Sihanna.

"Stay slow, fall behind. It's gonna be a long time before I get to hit Mirsinneen. I can get the Steel Snake now. You sure you can get that thing?"

Athena turned her head. With a big grin, she nodded. *"Yeah."*

"Let's go get it."

Athena turned the bike around. *"I can get a link from here."*

As they turned around, Mira sent a message, "What are you doing, Sihanna?"

Sihanna ignored it. "Are you in, Athena?"

"Yeah, the key is still good. Hang on—"

The Steel Snake stopped firing, turned around, and came back to the water. It splashed down, throwing up waves, steaming and hissing, then rolled onto the top of the tanks in front of Sihanna. It lay there, motionless.

Athena stopped the bike nearby. *"Alright. I've got it...holding...yeah, just stopped."*

"Sihanna, we need to go," Mira messaged.

"It's stopped. It's safe for now," Sihanna replied and looked back.

She had chased the Steel Snake back past their encampment. In the distance, she saw Mira and Damien's bikes turn around.

Damien messaged, "Si, our part is done. We can go home now."

Sihanna's lips curled down, her stomach filled with bitterness and despair. Loneliness, desperate loneliness filled her heart.

Go home. Without Allie?

She checked her display. The Steel Snake's temperature was dropping; there was no motion.

Mira stopped her bike beside Sihanna. "Sihanna, we need to go. Reinforcements will be here shortly. They have the tech to deal with this. There's nothing left for us to do here. We need to get to safety."

Sihanna looked at Mira and nodded. She messaged Athena silently, "How far away can you maintain contact with the Steel Snake?"

"I can relay through the battle bots, if necessary."

"Let's head back. Stay in contact with the Steel Snake. Find a way to destroy it."

Athena turned back again and grinned. *"You got it!"*

Sihanna pulled her goggles up and her hood down. She reached behind her neck, pulled her tiara off its attachment, and put it on top of her head. As she sped away, Sihanna put her hand on her upper chest, trying to feel her locket. She felt the tears flooding her eyes.

"Athena, I can't cry now."

She put her hood back up and pulled down her goggles.

"Got it."

They will pay, Allie, they will all die, Sihanna thought as memories of swimming a few days ago came back. *This used to be such a nice place.*

The bike shook as Sihanna heard an explosion behind her. "Athena, what's going on?"

"Huh…hang on…I think, ahh…yeah…something's happening."

"There's explosions going off all around! WHAT'S happening?"

"The Steel Snake did a…ahh…restart, I guess, and now I'm locked out."

More explosions erupted in front of and beside Sihanna's speeding bike. One hit too close and her bike flipped, airbags deployed, and the bike slid to a stop on its side. Sihanna pulled the emergency release and the canopy popped off. She climbed out as Mira and Damien slowed to a stop beside her.

"Si. You okay?" Damien broadcast.

"Yeah, fine."

Mira slid her canopy back. "Get on."

Before Sihanna could get on Mira's bike, another nearby explosion knocked her down.

"ATHENA!"

"Working on it."

Sihanna picked up her gun. *Spray will block its sensors.*

The targeting system came on in her display. The Steel Snake was moving, White flames shot from its *tail* as it turned for another firing run. Several red spots flashed in Sihanna's display. She kept her gun moving around, aiming at the red spots, but they disappeared before she could fire...then one held in place.

She pulled the trigger. The gun kicked back on her shoulder. She held the burst until the red spot disappeared. The Steel Snake fired two laser shots, then stopped. Another red spot appeared in Sihanna's display. She fired. This time the Steel Snake only got off one shot. Three more times Sihanna stopped it from firing a volley.

"SIHANNA!" Mira yelled over the link. "We have to go!"

"Athena! Do something. I'm out of ammo, gotta reload." Sihanna snapped the empty magazine out, dropped it, spun her backpack around the front as she knelt on one knee and reached in for a reload.

The Steel Snake started firing again. This time all energy was put into one powerful blast. A loud roar filled the air.

"ATHENA!"

Another explosion sent more dust and debris into the air.

"SIHANNA!" Mira had dismounted her bike and rushed through the swirling clouds of dust. "Sihanna. It's blasted a hole in the hab." Another large explosion sounded, followed by the awful sound of groaning metal and the roar of escaping atmosphere. "Sihanna, the hab's coming apart. We have to get out of here!"

The wind increased, pushing Mira along as she tried to see through the dust. Then she saw an infrared signature, a Human shape.

"Damien. I found her!"

"On my way."

Mira rushed to Sihanna's side and knelt beside her. "Jenny, can you contact Athena?"

"No response."

Another loud metallic groan sounded. Mira saw a large crack forming ahead, in Damien's direction. "Damien! Get to your bike, back to the warehouse. I've got Sihanna."

The crack grew fast, spreading across the tanks to the water. The water rushed into the tanks through the crack. The wind howled fiercely.

"Jenny, I'm gonna need my feet."

The armour slippers curled down over Mira's feet; they came off with her shoes when she kicked them off. The surface under her was beginning to tilt. The large section she was on was about to break away and be flung into space.

Mira cradled Sihanna in her arms and began running toward the crack. "Jenny, contact Gammarus."

Mira leaned into the wind and ran as fast as she could, her cyborg muscles working to full capacity. The bottom of her feet had microscopic fibres and used Van Der Waals force, one of the methods used by insects to walk on walls and ceilings; her feet wouldn't slip no matter how hard she ran.

"He's online, but—"

The surface tilted more as Mira approached the widening crack. "A couple more steps."

She jumped the last two steps, landed, crouched, and sprang back into a run.

Gammarus' avatar showed in Mira's display, giggling hysterically. Between giggles, he said, "Oh, it's Mira…he Hehe…Marshall Thabiti…hahaha."

"Gammarus, the hab is breaking up, eject your node! Get out!"

"Hehehe…hab breaking up, he Hehe—"

"He's high on emotion," Jenny messaged.

"Can you eject him?"

"Yes, hold on…okay, got it…being flung away from the debris. He should be safe."

Damien was waiting near the bikes, parked beside one of the tent enclosures. He ran to Mira when he saw her approach. The Steel Snake fired another volley, destroying the bikes. There was more loud groaning as the wind increased. Only the wall of the tent enclosure, serving as a windbreak, saved Mira and Damien from blown toward the holes.

Three silver human-form figures with rocket packs extending from their shoulders flew in and landed beside Mira and Damien. When they pulled down their hoods, the rocket packs folded in over the shoulders. The silver coating disappeared and became a cloak.

Three Elves stood there in black cotton pants and white shirts. The silver cloaks tied around their shoulders and hung down their backs, the hoods hanging loosely behind their heads. Mira handed Sihanna to Damien and one of the Elves tossed Mira a backpack.

"Need your toys when you go on vacation." He smiled and nodded toward Damien. "You need to get him to Ronin Six. We'll take care of things here."

All three then put up their hoods, the cloaks wrapped around their bodies, and covered them in a form-fitting silver coating. Rocket packs extended from their shoulders. They jumped into flight, chasing the Steel Snake.

One of them broadcasts, "You need to get out of here. Radiation's about to get lethal. Aurelianus is waiting for you with Ethie."

Mira opened the backpack. Inside was a silver cloak. She put it on and pulled the hood over her head. The cloak flowed around her body and she was covered with silver, a rocket pack extended from each shoulder.

"Hold onto Sihanna."

Damien nodded. Mira wrapped her arms around Damien and Sihanna. The rockets flared to life and she took flight. In the distance, the Elves were chasing the Steel Snake, shooting as they flew around and beside it. One of them landed on top of the tanks and a bright white light began to shine from him. The stone brick turned red; it started turning white as Mira flew through a hole in the habitat floor and then into space.

Pieces of the habitat were falling off, being flung by the spin and pushed by the escaping atmosphere. Large sections tumbled about as Mira navigated around the deadly debris. The ring had broken completely across its width and the ends started to flare out. Bigger and bigger sections began breaking off.

Dozens of balloon bots were moving to intercept the debris before it could damage another habitat. Ahead was Ethie, a Currie class destroyer, slowly spinning.

A sphere with disks facing front and back. Each disk was capped with four pylons that met to form a pyramid and held the white-hot glowing ball of the fusion reactors at its peak. In a few minutes, they were on board. Mira pulled down the hood, and the silver coating formed back into a cloak.

"We're getting out of here," Ethie broadcast as Damien and Mira make their way to the med lab.

Momentary sloping of the floors indicated Ethie was increasing acceleration too fast, but it quickly levelled.

In the med lab, Damien put Sihanna in a life pod, pulled up her goggles, and closed the pod. A white liquid oozed from the bottom and covered Sihanna in a form-fitting layer.

Results from the body scan showed in Mira's display. Her lips frowned deeply, tears building in her eyes.

"She was too close to the blast," she told Damien, quietly. "The shock damaged all the cells in her body at once, knocked out her med bots...and her PAL."

Mira rubbed her forehead with her hand. *Why, Sihanna? All you had to do was leave. WHY DIDN'T you JUST leave?*

She felt the tears building again but wiped her wet eyes before the tears could roll down her cheeks.

Damien stared at Sihanna.

Chapter 10

"Gauntlet has sent a message," Jenny messaged Mira.

"Hold on," she messaged back silently and heard footsteps behind her.

She turned around and saw Aurelianus a few steps away. He looked exactly like the bot but for a long scar on his right cheekbone, trailing down and disappearing into his beard.

"Tiz a shame we godda meet like dis," he said and embraced Mira in a brief hug.

"Ohh, it's been too long, Half Ton. Damn, bot fooled me too easy. Should've known soon as its PAL told me you'd healed your scar."

He rubbed his scar with a finger and nodded his head. "Well…you know full well I've thought about it." He shook his head. "More'n once." He looked at Damien and nodded. "How ya doin', laddie? I'm Aurelianus, call me Half Ton." He embraced Damien with a few pats on the back.

Damien gingerly put his arms around Aurelianus' large frame, then stepped back.

"Don't worry, Damien," Mira said. "This is the real Half Ton." She felt a lump in her throat and tried to smile. "He'll never turn against us."

"Yeah. Seen da video," Aurelianus said, shaking his head. "Wish I da been dere. Das one time I'd a liked kickin' some ass." He punched a fist into his hand.

Mira silently messaged Damien, "Are you okay?"

"Yeah. It's just…last time we saw Half Ton—"

"I feel it, too. We just have to remember it was a physical avatar of the Steel Snake that shot Allie, not the real Half Ton."

"Yeah, he was a pleasant travelling companion," Damien said as he looked at Aurelianus. "I hope we get to know the real Half Ton."

"Me too, laddie, me too," Aurelianus nodded.

Mira said, "Damien, Ethie can guide you to quarters and we can get changed. We won't need our armour."

"Okay. I'll meet you back here in an hour."

Aurelianus cleared his throat. "I'll meet up wit' ya fer supper."

Mira went to her quarters. "Jenny, let me see the message from Gauntlet."

"She was requesting contact as soon as convenient."

"Okay. Link with her."

An image of a female Elf appeared in Mira's display, dressed in black cotton pants and a dark red shirt, seated in a leather chair beside a small table with a teapot and cup, a bookshelf behind her. "It's good to see you, Mira."

"And you." Mira could feel her stomach beginning to boil. "And how is everyone on the Defence Council sleeping?"

Gauntlet, a CI from the earliest days of the Imperial Concordant, held the senior seat on the Defence Council. "We won't be able to save Homarus Habitat, but, with some help from the Elves, the balloon bots will be able to contain the debris. No other habitats will be damaged." She paused and took a sip from the cup. "We've found and contained, Steel Snakes in two other Dyson swarms. Still looking in others…looks like Mirsinneen already has forces in place to start a war, forces at some of our most vulnerable points."

"You're certain it's Mirsinneen? And you've ignored my question."

"Yes. War swarms have already been detected at several points along the wall. It's no longer a question, the war has begun…and Mirsinneen has been preparing for a long time."

Mira felt the boil in her stomach grow. "Yeah," she said with extreme sarcasm, "a long time. And we didn't know?"

"How could we? The attack on Aalya was the first clue."

"Thousands of tonnes moving about Homarus Habitat for at least twenty-two years and you expect me to believe it was undetected."

"What evidence shows it's been here for so long?" Gauntlet sipped from her teacup.

"It had Damien's DNA. The last time he was here was twenty-two years ago."

"There are agents everywhere. You fought them on Lutetia. They could have recorded his DNA at any time in the last twenty-two years."

"So, you know they've been on Lutetia for so long?"

Gauntlet sipped her tea again. "That was not the intent of my statement."

"BULLSHIT!" Mira's voice became a growl. "You, and the entire Defence Council, knew this attack was coming and you let it happen!"

"You're letting your emotions interfere with your judgment and erroneously making some very serious accusations."

"Please make sure the entire Defence Council knows of my accusations; I'll send you my feelings file to go with it. And where was this—" Mira tugged at the hood of her cloak, her voice again lowered to a growl, "When I got here? Those two girls didn't have to die."

"It's regrettable—"

"REGRETTABLE! If I had this cloak, they would be alive."

"All Shadow Watch will now have their cloaks at all times. Okay?" Gauntlet raised her eyebrows and sipped.

Stay calm, and breathe, in…out, Mira thought and then said, quietly, "About time…what's going to happen to Damien? I will remind you he is a free citizen. Let's not forget he has rights."

"Never. But he is currently serving in the Imperial Defence Force, with the rank of Commander and top secret security clearance. He has been assigned to Ronin Six for further training. We'll need you to take him there as soon as possible and then I'll need you to go to Tukulti Ashur. Prepare that section of the wall for when the war swarms arrive."

"You've detected the war swarms from Tukulti Ashur?"

"Yes. A large one headed directly there."

"As I recall from our simulations, if you've detected the swarms from Tukulti Ashur, then you detected them from Abzu Ashur over a year ago. At about the same time, Aalya was murdered. And you didn't know the attack was coming?" Then, with a rhetorical voice, she added, "The war has begun, henceforth let no truth be told." With that, she thought, *Just let it go. Not worth the stress now.* "Can't hide the destruction of this hab. Everyone will know the war has started, and that you knew it was coming. You, and the entire Defence Council, will have to explain some time."

"This will be explained as a terrorist attack. The Mirsinneen swarms won't arrive for two or three years. The war won't really start till then. The two events won't be linked. And with the DNA from the Aurelianus bot, we know what to look for and we'll have all the agents contained in a few months."

Mira closed her eyes and took a deep breath. "Of course. And the war at Uruk Ashur? Evacuation orders went out fast. Little more than a year since it started. What can I expect there?"

Gauntlet sipped her tea, then sighed a deep breath. "Mira, you have a mission. You need to take Damien to Ronin Six."

Mira felt the frustration boiling again *I guess I'll know when I **need** to know* she thought, then said, "First, we're going to Udara and then Lutetia!"

Gauntlet pursed her lips and nodded. "Of course. How can I refuse?" She smiled wryly. "You'll just cut communications, use your rank to *commandeer* a ship again and run off on your own adventure."

"That wasn't much of an adventure. What about the Elves? What are they doing here? Are they going to actually help this time?"

"Not certain yet. They volunteered a colony ship in the Shylow system when Aurelianus needed to get here quickly."

"Yeah…three days. Do we have that tech?"

Gauntlet shook her head. "It's just high acceleration."

"Not a colony ship, not that fast."

"The Elves have Q-tech. Of course, they can accelerate that fast."

"Are the Elves going to fight?"

"One of their colony fleets has requested discussions. We'll meet next month. Their ship at Har Megiddon is going to stay for now. Available if needed."

Mira took a deep breath, trying to release some tension with the exhale. "And when the fight starts, we're not gonna hold back this time. Hit 'em hard, and then hit 'em again. Everything we've got. Destruction in this war will be the worst we've seen. Let's do everything we can to make it short. This time the soldiers fight the war and the politicians can shut up and watch."

Gauntlet nodded. "We are a democratic society. The Military cannot make political decisions."

"In the last war, we had 'em down, our boot on its throat, and you pulled it back! We could have finished this a long time ago. Every person who dies in this war—"

"We made the best agreement possible at the time."

"When your enemy is down, you don't let him get back up!" Mira sighed, and shook her head. *Just leave it,* she thought, and asked "Anything else I need to know for now?"

"No. I'll send you an update on the defences at Tukulti Ashur. I've already ordered new ships and defence swarms to be built. Add anything you think you might need. You've got whatever resources the system has. Let me know if you need more. There's a wormhole there so I can get you anything you might need quickly."

Mira nodded. "Bye, for now."

"There can only be victory in this war. If Mirsinneen gets the upper hand…well, do whatever you need to do to stop 'em." Gauntlet sipped her tea. "Bye for now." The link closed.

Mira took off her armour, washed her face, and changed into a fresh uniform.

"Jenny, check and see if Damien is ready."

"He is. Skolto and Amboso have sent condolence messages."

"Send them greetings and thank you. Are they staying here?"

"They've requested a link."

"Link them." In Mira's view, two kittens appeared lying on a couch, one striped, orange and white, with a sliver A on its forehead, the other, white with black spots and a silver S on its forehead. Mira smiled. "New avatars?"

The white and black kitten sat up, and without moving its mouth said, "Yes. We plan to do some travelling, and explore the wormhole network for a while." The white and black kitten looked at the orange kitten, then turned back.

"We thought these avatars would be…cute." He meowed and smiled.

Mira smiled. "They are. Safe travels, Skolto."

"And you, Mira. We transferred everything you had onboard to the Raccoon it's headed your way on autonavigation. 'Til we meet again."

The link closed. Mira checked herself in the mirror, took a deep breath, and then went back to the med lab. Damien was already there, dressed in the same uniform as Mira, holding the scissors. He opened the life pod. The white coating had retracted.

Sihanna was still wearing her armour, the goggles up and the hood pulled back, her long hair sticking out. Damien reached inside the pod, cut off a lock of hair, and handed the scissors to Mira. She cut off a lock of hair while Damien put his in his locket.

Mira handed the scissors back to Damien. He put them back in Sihanna's handbag and hung the handbag off his left shoulder. He leaned into the pod and kissed Sihanna on the forehead. Mira did the same.

Chapter 11

Damien sat on the ground, beside his father's freshly filled grave. He fiddled with the lock of hair. He picked up his locket lying on the ground beside his foot, opened it, and pressed his father's lock of hair into it.

It's full, he thought and tried to close it. *Even hard to close.* He let it flip open again, looked at the locks of hair, and counted them off.

Mom…Mal…Allie…Si…Dad.

He pressed hard to close it. He slipped it into his pocket and walked a short distance through the orchard park and came to a clearing with a log cabin. Malik's cabin. He walked to the cabin and stepped onto the low deck. He was greeted by a grey-striped kitten, with a silver K on its forehead, excitedly running around, jumping and rubbing against his leg.

Damien smiled and grinned. "Hey, Cutie Katie. How ya doin'?" He bent down and petted her.

She excitedly licked his fingers.

She followed Damien into the cabin, running in and out of the open door several times.

Lotta good memories here, Damien thought.

He looked around and a wave of sadness washed over him. Memories flooded his mind. *Lotta happy times here. He remembered parties with Sihanna and Allie singing and dancing, Malik dancing wildly to upbeat dance music, many other friends, lots of drinking, eating, laughing, playing games…*

Katie stood in the doorway, looked back and forth, looked back at Damien, hopped about, and meowed. She ran out the door and outside a couple of steps, looked about, then looked back at Damien and meowed. She ran back inside and looked about. She ran outside again, looked all around, meowed, looked at Damien, looked around again, came back inside and looked up at Damien.

Damien bent down and held his hand close to the floor, palm up. Katie ran and jumped into his hand.

"No, Katie…it's just you and me," he said as he stood.

He held Katie close to his face and she began licking the tears rolling down his cheeks.

"No one else is coming home."

Background and Inspiration

The emotional experience of a traumatic event, such as natural disaster or death of a loved one, can be the beginning of a life changing emotional journey. Har Megiddon explores the emotional trauma of wartime with Damien and his party.

In the first chapter, Damien's father is murdered, and he and his friends have to run for their lives. They feel shock and confusion, like that felt at the beginning of a war. In their desperate run for safety, they have to steal a car. At the outbreak of war, nations will be scrambling to mobilize all available assets, old and obsolete equipment will be put into service, civilian manufacturing retooled to produce military equipment, long retired veterans will be called back to service. The war may have been expected, but surprise and fear will reign when the shooting starts. And when *all* news could be misinformation, confusion will join the chaos.

Damien's friends are by his side, without question. Blind loyalty to their friend. Many who volunteered during both World Wars did so out of a sense of patriotism. They went to war, solely, 'for King and country', with little regard for consequences. Malik's emotional upheaval while looking for a car to steal mirrors that felt by everyone affected, directly and indirectly, by war.

As they prepare to leave Lutetia, Damien and Malik are excited about the prospect of flying a ship they've used in games, and visiting some historic parts of the Empire. Many wartime volunteers would be visiting ancestral homelands. They would be experiencing new technology such as flight, radar, and sonar. Some technology unknown, some seen only in movies.

Malik, the first to die, the civilian adventurer, rushes to battle, unprepared. Many wartime volunteers were expecting adventure. They volunteered out of patriotism and expected to come home after a glorious victory. A horde did not return.

The party experiences grief with Malik's death. The inexperienced civilian, excited about the coming adventure, is the first of Damien's friends to die. The death of a comrade is a near certainty when serving during wartime, along with the threat of death at any time.

When they arrive at Har Megiddon, the party gets to enjoy some of the local entertainment. When deployed away from home, soldiers will enjoy a night out, at every possible opportunity. Allie and Sihanna's close relationship means they give each other support. Many close friends, or relatives volunteered together, vowing to 'look after each other'. As long as they are together, everything will be fine. Mira's discussion about one of her worst experiences, depicts the effect war and its horrors can have on people and their attitude toward life and law.

Rocket fuel is real. The mixture of one quarter water and three quarters alcohol was used as fuel on the Redstone rocket, which launched the first United States astronaut into space. On twenty first century Earth the mixture is more well known as moonshine.

When they prepare to go on a scouting mission Allie feels the fear of battle. "Anybody who says they weren't scared was lying, or crazy." was stated by many D-Day veterans. All soldiers feel afraid when going to battle. Some will check their weapon and ammunition a few times while waiting. And there is often, too much waiting. For the religious, there's time for lots of praying.

When Mira realizes the full extent of what's happening, she takes command and has to engage in the old debate between government and military, about war, politics and economics.

Food on the front lines can be a challenge. Hundreds of years ago soldiers had to forage for their own food as they marched. This often meant 'acquiring' from farms and merchants along the way. Field rations are served to soldiers in the field today are a vast improvement over those in the past. The famous hard biscuits of World War One could crack teeth if not soaked first.

When the enemy is encountered, they have weapons Damien and party have no defence against. War has seen the introduction of many new weapons. Today we have drone swarms and cyber attacks. Nuclear weapons were used during World War Two. During World War One, submarines, aircraft, tanks and gas were new. Gas was feared most.

Harold Mathews reported:

"It is impossible for me to give a real idea of the terror and horror spread among us by this filthy loathsome pestilence. It was not, I think, the fear of death or anything supernatural but the great dread that we could not stand the fearful suffocation…"

Alfred West saw some of the injured.

They were trying to drink some water out the side of the road. And they were almost visibly blowing up – their bodies were going coloured, but they were blowing up. You could put your finger and make a little hole, almost, in them… the water wasn't good and they were lying down, getting down and drinking it but that was the worst thing they could do. But there was nothing else they could do.

Jack Dorgan was injured during a gas attack.

"Our eyes were streaming with water and with pain. Luckily again for me I was one of those who could still see. But we had no protection, no gas masks or anything of that kind. All we had was roll of bandages from our first aid kit."

The Aurelianus bot, posing as a friend, commits the ultimate act of betrayal and kills Allie. Sihanna's grief is unbearable, Allie was her life, now she's gone. Many close friends and relatives volunteered for service together. When one fell, the survivor would often fall into a pit of despair, and never get out. Allie's injuries were horrific, as are many during battle. The sights, smells and sounds of combat, with wounded and dead all around, has left all veterans with fearsome memories, and more than a few nightmares.

Sihanna feels guilty about Malik and Allie's deaths, her thirst for vengeance fixates her on an impossible quest. When she simply had to run to get to safety, vengeance comes first. She dies needlessly, the last of Damien's friends to die, their reward for their loyalty.

Mira and Damien are left in a precarious position, but the timely arrival of reinforcements gives them a chance to retreat. Mira's conversation with Gauntlet discusses politics, the role of military during war, and the constant use of misinformation. The old warrior argues, but the Empire is ultimately in command. The discussion about the treaty the ended the Mirsinneen war is a reference to the treaty that ended World War One. Ferdinand Foch, Supreme Allied Commander at the end of the war described it a twenty year armistice (a temporary cessation of hostilities). World War Two began twenty years and ten months later.

Throughout their quest, Damien and his party are constantly striving to get reliable information, or any information to help them understand what's happening around them. Accurate knowledge of an area and all obstacles is necessary to plan or execute an operation. For the soldiers involved, accurate updates on the ongoing situation are required. Having access to trustworthy information and news reports can be a challenge in everyday life. Social media gives us an unprecedented ability for dissemination and discussion of ideas. Our increased ability to communicate also provides a platform for intentional acts of spreading false and misleading information.

When Damien returns home to bury his father, he reflects on the true cost of war.